Romance & Vampires

BOOK 2

GINGER LEE

Editor Brandi Zelenka

My Notes in the Margin

www.mynotesinthemargins.com/

Cover design by Angela Haddon

Cover Photographer Christopher John

CJC Photography

www.cjc-photography.com/

Printed in the United States of America

Paperback ISBN 979-8-9885489-0-4

Ebook ISBN 978-1-7350544-9-0

Author's Website: www.gleewrites.com

 Created with Vellum

Romance & Vampires

GINGER LEE

One

MICAH

"Let's go home." The sweetest words I'd ever heard. And she thought I was beautiful. Not a threat. Not a monster. Willa still loved me, and it was the best feeling in the world.

AFTER LEAVING the old Ursuline Convent and Cateline's pile of ashes behind in the fireplace, Jacque took Leona to a holding cell who knows where and Thomas said he was ready to hibernate for a long while. Harris, Trace, Alder, Willa, and I went back to Willa and Trace's home. Well, it was my home now, too.

The sun would soon be rising, so we all went around securing the shutters. We were amped up with adrenaline and no one was ready to rest just yet. Trace opened her best wine. She beamed as she poured five stemless glasses full, emptying the bottle.

"What a night. I can't believe our plan went off without a hitch." Harris clinked his glass with hers and kissed her cheek.

Alder rubbed Willa's back as she stood beside me. Our arms were touching, and I noticed she was staring at me when I looked down at her.

"Damn, you act like you've never seen me before."

She went on her tiptoes and pressed a gentle kiss on my cheek. "I'm sorry. I can't help it." Then she sniffed my shoulder. "Hmm. Whipped cream...or...marshmallow cream. I wondered what you would smell like. You vampires have your own unique smells, you know. And yours is yummy." She smelled me again. I could only laugh. I instantly got turned on, but this wasn't the time for sex. Yet. I leaned further down with my nose in her hair and whispered into her ear. "And I'll have a taste of you soon enough."

Alder knew what steamy scenarios were running through our minds. He reached over and squeezed my shoulder with a wink. "There is a lot to be learned, Micah. You had your fill tonight, but soon the hunger pain will return. We will rest here today. At dusk, you and I have a little training to do."

Willa whipped her head towards Alder. "Training? And what does that involve?"

Harris smiled. "He'll probably need a good week or two to gain control of his thirst. Maybe more. Our appetites can be monstrous at first."

"*Two weeks*?" I exclaimed. "I can't leave for two weeks. I've only just returned to Willa." I possessively wrapped my arms around her shoulders from behind.

Alder shook his head. "There's no need in arguing. You won't win. We *will* be gone. And it will be for however long I deem necessary. Believe me, you would never forgive yourself if you harmed her."

Willa rubbed her hands over my forearms. "I guess it has to be done." She sighed.

"Where will you go?" asked Trace.

"Maybe London," suggested Harris.

I scoffed. "That far?"

"Yes, that far," Alder confirmed. "It's the ideal place. After a while, when I feel you are ready, Harris will bring Trace and Willa. You all will meet the clutch there. David Kingswood is the primus. You've probably heard of him."

Trace's jaw dropped. "Oh my god. The *famous* David Kingswood? Of Kingswood Talent?"

I couldn't believe it either. "You mean to tell me he's a vampire? He's been my idol since the beginning of my career. Still is. I had no idea. How did I not know this?"

Alder laughed. "I know, it's hard to believe. He's a young vampire, but he embraced the lifestyle with such ease. It came naturally. You know David's modeling career has always been successful. When he turned thirty, he had a great desire to become one of us. The primus of London at the time was his business partner, Ian, so David had a great understanding of what being a true vampire entailed. Ian had been primus for over a century and wanted to start traveling a bit. The clutch overwhelmingly approved David's takeover. He's designing a new fashion line that's darker and more gothic than what he has built his reputation on. You'll see, Micah. I think you'll love it."

"I have a feeling the world will know his secret soon enough. It's going to be a big deal," Harris added. He massaged the back of Trace's neck. "We're going to have so much fun in London. I can't wait to take you," he said into her ear.

I started to move away from Willa, but she latched on, keeping my arms tightly around her, and pressed her back into my chest. "Don't," she pleaded.

I whispered into her ear. "I'm here. I've got you."

She turned to Alder. "I'd love to have a few minutes alone with Micah."

He nodded. "Of course."

Willa pulled me to her room. As soon as she shut the door, she jumped into my arms and we held each other. I leaned back to see tears running down her face. "What's this? Don't cry." I kissed her salty cheeks.

"I'm so sorry. I'm sorry for everything. We didn't keep you

safe and..." I covered her mouth with mine. I held her so tight against my chest and kissed her like it would be the last time, but I knew there would be so many more. I wanted to take away her pain. Her body vibrated with energy. Energy she needed to release. I pulled back and held her beautiful face.

"Willa, close your eyes and breathe slowly. Listen to me. None of it was your fault. It wasn't Alder's either. Cateline is gone. I'm right here. I'm right here." I kissed her again, hard and long. Her energy pervaded my being, making me feel very much the same as when I had been glamoured, and my fangs descended. I pulled back, embarrassed again. "Sorry, I'll control it one day. I promise."

The look of love in Willa's eyes gave me confidence. It was true. I didn't have a choice, but in that moment, I felt invincible. Not because I was immortal, but because I belonged to Willa. And the energy between us felt magnified now. I could see why a true vampire would desire her more than other humans. She buried her face in my chest. "Thank you for being alive. I was so afraid of them killing you. If you ever want to talk about it, I'll be here to listen. But I understand if you want to bury it and never speak of it again."

I squeezed her tight as a light knock came from the door, drawing our attention. "Yes," I said.

Alder peeked his head in. "May I come in?"

There he was. The other part of me. "Yes, of course."

He sat on Willa's bed. "Everything alright? Do either of you need anything?"

"Some rest would be nice," Willa replied. Alder turned off the lights, leaving the lamp on, and started to undress. I helped Willa out of her clothes, then shed mine. She slid into the middle of her queen size bed, and we climbed in on both sides. Willa snuggled into Alder's chest, and I spooned her from behind. Alder smiled at me over her head, and it filled me with bliss. Our eyes glowed at one another, and I reached to hold his hand on her hip.

When Willa's breaths came deep from sleep, Alder whispered.

"It's going to be hard to leave her. And we just got you back. But I'm so thankful." He laced his fingers together with mine.

I sighed. "I guess now a few weeks is only a drop in the ocean, isn't it?"

He laughed quietly. "Right. I guess it is. Have you ever been to London?"

"I've been twice for modeling. Never for fun."

"Well then, I'll be sure to show you a very good time."

I grinned. I couldn't imagine the definition of fun for vampires.

Alder's playful grin straightened into a serious line. "The next few nights will be intense. In a few hours, the pains will return. I'm going to get you fed before that happens. And it won't be from Willa. You will have to train your body to recognize how much is too much and you will *only* enjoy Willa's blood for intimacy. Never out of the need to feed. That's why I won't let her join us until you are ready."

I didn't have a response. I knew Alder would end me if I ever harmed her, and I would want him to. He raised up and pulled me into a soft kiss with Willa securely between us. It was brief, but it felt like a promise that he would do everything in his power to protect our union. We laid back down with no more words and went to sleep.

Two

WILLA

My phone alarm went off at 5 pm. Micah reached over to silence it and went back to snoozing. I blinked and took in a deep breath through my nose, taking in the scent of my vampires. I had never slept so well. Alder opened his eyes and smiled. I melted and kissed him. "Good evening, Mr. Hunt."

He pulled my body flat against his. "Mmm, good evening, darling." We kissed some more and then Micah flipped over and his arm wound around my waist. His nose nuzzled my back. God, I would miss them.

Alder tucked my hair behind my ear. "He is so happy to be home. He loves you very much."

Micah's arm tightened. "Hell yes, I do," he sleepily grumbled.

We all laughed, and Micah propped up on one elbow to rub his eyes. I rolled onto my back and stretched in the tight space between them. Micah winced and touched his abdomen.

"We better get up, have some coffee, and say our goodbyes," Alder stated. "Harris is flying us to London tonight. We need to leave in about two hours and get you fed beforehand."

"So, you have your very own vampire jet," Micah joked.

"Indeed. Don't worry. Harris is an excellent pilot."

What a world I was living in. Life would be so different from now on. Micah kissed the back of my neck then paused and pulled back a little. I turned to look at him and his eyes were concerned. I knew we needed some space between us. Alder got out of the bed.

"Did you hear her heartbeat? Was it pounding in your ears? Willa's lifeforce flowing just under the surface, begging you to partake? That's natural, but it will only intensify the hunger. It's important you both know how serious it is to spend some time apart."

Micah quickly kissed my cheek and slid from behind me. "Yeah, that scared me for a second. No offense Willa, but I don't want to have you for dinner."

I laughed a little. "None taken." Alder disappeared into the closet then returned with my fluffy robe and tossed it to me. "You wouldn't happen to have an extra toothbrush, would you?"

Micah went into the bathroom en suite. "I have a ton. I keep them for traveling to modeling gigs." Alder followed him and when I joined them, they were standing together at the sink, brushing their teeth. It was quite a sight. I couldn't help but smile.

TRACE

I treasured every moment Harris and I spent together, sitting at the kitchen table and sipping coffee alone. He would be gone for a couple of days, but I was thankful he would be back after that short time. It was unknown how long it would take Alder to train Micah. Willa would probably be moping around the house for days.

Harris glanced at his watch. "Those three. I may have to go light a fire under them."

"Um, I don't think they need any help doing that," I laughed. "You may walk in on something scandalous."

Harris licked his lips. "Believe me, I've seen just about everything." I leaned closer for a toe-curling kiss.

He moaned and grasped a fist full of my red hair.

I moaned back as his mouth moved down my neck. "You'll have to educate me."

"There's a club in London. It takes vampire bar to another level. David Kingswood owns it. The clutch there runs it. He's tried to get Alder to open one here a million times, but he won't pull the trigger. Let's just say your wildest fantasy can be had there if you so choose."

"I don't even know what my wildest fantasy is, to be honest."

"Well, we can observe and see if anything tickles your fancy." Harris looked wicked. Alder, Micah, and Willa walked in together and grabbed coffee mugs. Micah's mouth was in a straight line, and he winced a little with his first sip of coffee. Harris patted his shoulder. "Nothing will feel quite right until you feed. We should head out in a few minutes. I was just telling Trace about the club in London."

"I hear it's quite the experience," I said.

"So? Tell me," Willa pushed.

Alder pondered his words. "It's hard to describe. There is a bar. There are dancing girls, dancing guys...private rooms to feed in and...to do other activities."

I knew he was holding back. "Harris mentioned observing?"

"You mean sexual acts," Willa bluntly stated.

Harris grinned. "Oh, yes."

Micah's fangs descended and he covered his mouth. "Damn, I'm sorry. I think I got a little excited. And I'm starving."

Willa put her arms around his waist and hugged him from behind as they shuffled toward the front door. "Go eat. I love you. I'll miss you more than you know."

He turned around for a short goodbye kiss. "The next time I see you, we'll make up for missed time, I promise."

"Meet me in the Jag." Alder tossed Micah the keys and he reluctantly left. Alder embraced Willa, grabbing her ass in front of me and Harris. "I love you, darling. Don't miss me too much." He started to move away when she stopped him.

"Wait." She pulled her hair over one shoulder and presented her neck. "A little for the road."

He leaned down and took her offering. After he had his taste, he licked the wound. His eyes glowed bright. "I'll text you when we arrive in London." Willa watched him step outside and dragged herself to the couch. The moping had already begun.

I walked onto the porch with Harris. Watching Alder and Willa turned me on, and he knew it. I placed my hand over his slow, steady heart and put his over mine. "It beats for you."

"I'll be back in two days. Bye, love." He kissed me and was gone.

I cuddled up next to my best friend. She pulled out her phone and was already texting Micah.

"What? I'm just telling him that I'm thinking about my vampires, and I miss them already and I hope they have safe travels."

I patted her knee. "You three are a love for the ages. I adore it." Her phone dinged with a fast response. "What'd he say?"

She laughed at me and paused, then sighed and read aloud. "Don't mope around the house too much. Enjoy your alone time because Alder and I are going to..." She put her hand over her mouth and gasped.

"What?!"

She quickly put her phone away. "I'll never tell."

Three

MICAH

The night air was crisp and cool, and I smelled fresh blood as soon as we entered Potions. Our bags were packed and waiting in the back of Alder's Jag to head out after the short stop to get me fed before the eight-hour trip. I followed Alder and Harris into a room usually reserved for tea leaf readings. A pretty girl with mahogany hair and glowing blue eyes brought three full bottles of deep red blood and Alder thanked her by name. Sable. I'm sure a human would never be allowed to serve a trio of hungry vampires. Especially including a very new vampire. The glass warmed my hand, and we clinked them together before drinking them down. The first drop took away the hunger pains.

Harris wiped his mouth with the back of his hand. "The weather is perfect. There shouldn't be any concerns for the entirety of the flight."

Sable returned with a basket. "The fruit and mineral water are packed as you requested." She lightly touched Alder's shoulder. "Is there anything else you would like, Mr. Hunt?"

He cleared his throat uncomfortably. "Thank you, Sable. Nothing else."

Harris wore a sly smile and leaned forward to explain after she left the room. "Sable has been very...gracious, in the past. It doesn't make it sound any better, but we only recently found our mates. Sable met some of our carnal needs."

I shook my head. "No. No, I understand. Uh, Willa and I, you know, we weren't together like that. There was a makeup artist I used to see. Before." I thought about it for a while. "It *is* a little fucked up that you both did the same chick."

Laughter erupted. Harris slapped his knee. "You're hilarious, mate. Don't worry. I'm not touching Willa."

"I'd end you," Alder growled with a smile on his face. He turned to me. "Feeling better? I can get you more if you want." He lifted his empty bottle.

"I think I'm good." My god, I wanted Alder in that moment. I wanted to crawl on top of him and...

Harris was on his feet and out the door in a blink. Alder read my mind and reached out a hand. I took it and he pulled me over. I straddled his lap and we kissed. He was slow and gentle at first. I rubbed my hard on against his flat abs. He was a great kisser. His moans drove me wild, and his mouth vibrated against my skin as he moved his lips down my neck. The way he gripped my hips, pressing me as close as he could, sent me over the edge. My hands raced to undo my pants and I came in my own palm. I panted and felt like I had done something wrong. I scrambled off his lap. "I'm so sorry. I don't know what came over me. I didn't get any on you, did I?"

I was beyond embarrassed. Alder took a napkin from the table and began to clean the cum from my palm. "Don't you dare apologize. You did nothing wrong. Being a vampire intensifies arousal. You will get used to it. I quite like driving you crazy." He smirked and winked, and I immediately felt at ease. "Let's get on that plane."

THE JET WAS IMMACULATE. I expected nothing less. Harris had control over various buttons and flashing lights. He flipped switches and smiled at me before closing the cockpit door. Alder and I sat in captain chairs. I reclined mine a little and Alder took a laptop from his duffle bag and scrolled through emails.

"I noticed the name of the plane is Invictus. That's from a famous poem, right?"

"Yes, it's very relevant to true vampires. The words mean a lot to our unconquerable souls."

"I get it. I *do* remember the gist of it, believe it or not. I like poetry."

Alder handed over the laptop then reached over and held one of my hands. "I know I didn't tell you that you would be studying during the trip, but we have about eight hours and the Vampire Collective is full of information for you to learn. Take your time. You don't have to soak it all in tonight."

"No, this is great." I clicked on the main menu and picked History, which was at the top of the list. "To be honest, I'm excited to know more. And I need to get my mind off of Willa... and the urge to climb back on top of the vampire who is holding my hand right now." Of course, he already knew what I was thinking.

WILLA

I was dreaming. I knew I was dreaming because my body floated against a ceiling. The room was dim, and a fire crackled in a beautifully carved stone fireplace. This wasn't my room or any room I had been in, but it *was* me laying in a bed on my side and watching the flickering flames. I was naked and Alder lay behind me with his head buried in a pillow. A feeling of contentment surrounded me. Alder propped up and placed his hand on my knee. He slowly slid it up my thigh, over my hip, then around to cup my breast and I moaned. I felt his nose and hot breath at the nape of my neck. "Mmm, Willa."

My heart stopped for a second. *That's not Alder.* I panicked a little. It wasn't Alder. And I knew it wasn't Micah, because the unknown man had thick dark hair and a British accent. *What. The. Fuck.*

I startled awake, panting. My heart raced and my body wanted sex. What in the hell was going on? I felt guilty for *not* feeling guilty. I sat up and opened the nightstand drawer. I took out my trusty tentacle vibrator, Hiddles. My kink for tentacles was something only Trace knew about me. Getting off was the quickest and easiest way to release the most energy, so Hiddles and I headed to the shower.

IT WAS 4 am when I found Trace awake and sitting on the couch hugging her mug of coffee. I was so thankful she was up and coffee was already made. I poured my own, adding two Splendas and vanilla creamer. She patted my knee when I sat beside her as she watched the news. After a few minutes and several sips of caffeine, she spoke.

"So, everything okay?"

I debated telling her about the dream but decided not to just yet. "I'll be fine."

My phone dinged. It was from Micah.

Hi love ;) We landed hours ago. The flight was fine. I learned a lot from the Vampire Collective site on the way to London. Alder said you should check it out. Anyway, we rested and are about to head out to Lust. That's the club we were talking about. Clever name, right? I'm only going to feed. Promise. I'll call you at a decent hour. XO

I replied.

Okay. You know I trust you. Kiss Alder for me. I love you both. Have fun. XOXO

"They're good."

"Yeah, Harris called me about an hour ago. He's heading back tomorrow."

"Lucky dog," I laughed.

Four

MICAH

David Kingswood's home was a renovated stately house near Richmond Park. The vampire who let us in, and who gave us a partial tour of the house, was not David. His name was Marco and he spoke as if he'd built the place with his own hands. The kitchen was ultra-modern with dark wood and white surfaces, while the rest of the rooms were comfortably eclectic. Furniture covered in jewel tones popped against navy blue walls. Design was something I had always been interested in and I was surrounded by beauty here.

A newfound instinct told me the sun was rising outside and I felt a twinge of hunger. Alder knew. He grabbed my hand as Marco escorted us into a large, dark bedroom. "There is warm, fresh blood on the desk. Get some rest and Mr. Kingswood will be back by the time you wake."

"Thank you, Marco," Alder said as he handed me a warm bottle. He tapped his against mine as my fangs descended. I turned it up and Alder touched his hand to mine, pulling the bottle back down.

"Lesson number one: don't rush. Take your time. Our bodily

functions run at a much slower pace. No need to be gluttonous. Teaching yourself to take your time casually drinking readily available blood will help you take it slow when you feed for pleasure. Understand?"

I took a small drink and let it saturate my mouth. It did taste better when I let myself enjoy it. "Yes. It makes sense." I still drank mine faster than Alder. I set the empty bottle back on the desk and kissed Alder's forehead before stripping and sliding under the purple duvet. I raised an eyebrow at him.

He laughed while he undressed and shook his head. "Not right now, Micah. Lesson number two: we rest during the day."

WILLA

I floated above a library or an office or something similar. I saw myself leaning against a desk. Seated behind it was David Kingswood. He looked annoyed. So did I. I felt the energy from us both.

"I'm not like this. I don't do this," he said through gritted teeth.

"What? Be vulnerable? Open yourself up to humans?"

He stood up quickly, hitting a fist on the desk, and roared, "No one! I...there's no one. There's never fucking been anyone. I don't get emotionally involved with humans or vampires."

Suddenly, I no longer floated above the scene. It was like I was there in real time. I flinched and tried not to let my fear show. I *was* afraid, though. I was unsure of what to say, but I wanted to appear strong. I was also getting increasingly irritated. "Then don't. I can leave." I turned to let myself out.

David was out from behind his desk and had grabbed my wrist before I had taken two steps. "No. Don't go." His grip was firm, but then he loosened it. His body was so close, and his nose sniffed the top of my head. He gently pulled my wrist up to his nose and smelled there too. He closed his eyes and heat throbbed between my legs. David Kingswood was potent, and I felt weak.

He tilted his head and whispered into my ear. "You make me weak too, Willa. And I secretly don't even mind that much. I just don't know what to do about it. And I don't know why I'm telling you exactly what I'm thinking and feeling, damnit."

"Do Alder and Micah know?"

He shifted back a step to look into my eyes. "They will soon enough."

My eyes opened as light flooded my room and I hated waking up. I wanted to know more. I wanted David Kingswood, and I missed Alder and Micah.

MICAH

Our host wasn't anywhere in his house when we stirred at dusk. "Don't be disappointed. We will see him at Lust soon enough. I imagine you're hungry again. Let's head out. No bottled blood tonight. You and I will have a private room and a very willing donor." He winked.

LUST LOOKED JUST as I imagined and Harris had described. The men and women dancing in cages were mesmerizingly beautiful and the music entrancing. My cock pressed against the zipper of my black jeans as I followed Alder past a long bar packed with patrons. He wasn't kidding about being aroused so easily. The counter of the bar ran parallel to the dancefloor where more good-looking people grinded against one another. Alder paused in front of a black door and turned to me. He held my face and kissed me, slipping his tongue into my mouth. I sucked on it and pressed our bodies together. His groans drove me wild. He ended the kiss and knocked on a door. A pretty human, who apparently recognized him, let us pass through. Alder took my hand and hers and led us down a hallway with more black doors on either side. I smelled her blood as we walked side by side behind him. She didn't look at me, but I stared at her until we entered a room that was obviously made for pleasure and maybe something sinister. It was small, dark, and one piece of furniture sat in the middle. A platform bed covered with plastic. Pillows and blankets were strewn on the floor. I wondered what gruesome acts took place in this room. Surely Alder and I weren't going to kill this girl here...

Alder released our hands and the girl sat on the edge of the bed. "Sometimes things can get messy. Don't worry. I don't fancy that. Aleksandra is only here as a donor and then she will be dismissed."

I sighed with relief. She scooted to the center of the mattress and reclined back to offer herself to us.

"Lesson number three: Learn when to stop." He laid next to her and touched the pulse at her throat, then gestured for me to join them. I climbed up on her other side. Her face turned toward Alder. Her neck looked delectable. "Remember your first lesson."

"Right. Take my time." My fangs had been out and ready since we entered Lust. I leaned closer to take in her scent. Aleksandra smelled like brown sugar bourbon. "Does everyone smell this good?"

Alder laughed a little. "No. We vet our donors well. Only the most delicious offerings are allowed. And health checks are done monthly. Go on. I won't let you hurt her."

She held Alder's gaze, but spoke softly to me, "I trust you, Micah." With her words, I gently pricked her hot flesh and let my lips mold to the curve of her neck. She tasted divine and I thought about Willa.

Alder's soothing voice was in my ear. "Very good. You are doing well, Micah. Keep going. You can have a bit more."

I let myself suck a little deeper.

"Listen to her heartbeat. That steady beat will let you know if your donor is relaxed and trusting. You will know if a donor becomes afraid or uncomfortable. The pulse quickens. The donors are trained just like new vampires. They are not here to be sexually aroused, which almost always elevates their pulse."

I stopped sucking but kept my mouth on Aleksandra. I closed my eyes and listened to her heart. I could sense her mood as well and she seemed content. I did too. I pulled my lips away and licked the marks I had made like Alder did for Willa and myself. When I looked at him, he nodded in approval.

I rolled onto my back next to Aleksandra. She sat up and kissed Alder's cheek before kissing mine and then she left. "Thank you," I called after her as she closed the door.

Alder started unbuttoning his shirt. "You are amazing, Micah. So gentle and kind. It's of the utmost importance to be gentle and kind with donors. It comes naturally to you. Your training may be easier than I had anticipated."

When he shed his pants and briefs, he was as turned on as I was. I got out of my jeans and t-shirt as fast as I could. I wished Willa was with us. He propped up over me and reached down to stroke my cock. "I wish she was here too." He kissed my neck and then made his way down my chest. I held myself back from rushing. I wanted him to consume me. I needed it. I groaned as Alder took all of me into his mouth. He knew what he was doing. Oral sex had never felt so good. I grunted, about to come. I tried to pull out of his mouth, and he grabbed my hips, holding me in place. I let myself go completely and panted with release. When I opened my eyes, Alder had gotten himself off and glistening cum dripped onto the plastic covering the bed. His eyes looked seductive and wickedly pleased. He climbed up to let me taste his lips again before we dressed. Kissing Alder felt so different than kissing Willa, and I was lucky to have them both.

"Now what?" I asked, secretly hoping to finally meet David Kingswood. Alder knew what I wanted.

"Now, if we can find him, we meet the owner of this fine establishment."

Five

MICAH

We exited the room and moved further down the hall, away from the main club. A goldleaf door stood at the end. A large, muscled bouncer nodded a hello to Alder. "Mr. Kingswood isn't in his office," he informed us in a British accent that was much thicker than Harris or Alder's.

"Bloody hell. Where is he?"

The man shrugged. "Somewhere in the club. Fancy trying the bar."

Alder huffed, turned on his heel, and briskly headed in that direction. I knew he was annoyed.

"Is something wrong?"

"I'm wondering why David's being so elusive."

Aleksandra opened the door for us, and Alder scanned the crowd. I spotted David speaking to another vampire sitting on a barstool. He had been a super model for over fifteen years and seeing him in the flesh, I understood why he would want to become a vampire. David was perfect. He would remain perfect forever. The woman's eyes glowed as he whispered into her ear.

Alder and I leaned on the bar and waited for him to notice us. When he did, he looked surprised and uncomfortable. He smiled but ran a hand nervously through his hair.

"Alder Hunt. How long's it been, mate?"

They shook hands and Alder put an arm around my waist, pulling me to his side. "This is Micah Laroi. He's my mate and a successful model back in the states."

David oozed sex appeal and he clasped my hand and held it. "I'm chuffed to meet you. I trust your accommodations are to your liking? And vampire life is all new to you, am I right?"

"Very. And yes, but Alder is a great teacher."

He released my hand and looked sincere. "I know this wasn't of your choosing either. I can't imagine. And I'm sorry that some of our kind treated you that way. Good riddance to those bitches."

I couldn't help but laugh. "It's okay. I would die over and over again for Willa or Alder."

Something moved across David's face when I mentioned Willa's name. He cleared his throat. "If you both will excuse me, I won't be long."

Alder surprised me when he grabbed David's arm. "Hold on a minute. We need to talk. Are you avoiding us? I feel like you are."

David sighed and looked into Alder's eyes. "Not here. My office."

He paced the floor for a minute then sat in the chair behind his desk. "Please, sit."

Alder cocked his head. "This is serious, innit?"

David leaned forward on his elbows and steepled his fingers. "It's about Willa." Then silence.

"Well, out with it. What about our Willa?"

I kept my mouth shut. I was the new, inexperienced vampire and I knew my place around them, but I grew concerned the longer we waited for David to explain.

"I've been dreaming of her."

Alder frowned and he fisted his hands on his knees. "Come again?"

"I'm sorry. I can't help it! I can't control my dreams, now, can I? I don't know why it's happening."

David looked sincerely bewildered, as did Alder, as he tried to process the information. Alder stood and leaned to place his hands firmly on David's desk. "Now, just what exactly happens in these dreams of yours?"

The words passed over David's lips like it was painful to speak. "I...we...talk. I tell her things. Things I've never confessed to anyone else." Then his voice softened. "She soothes my spirit and makes my world a brighter place, even if it *is* only in dreams. Even if I know she isn't mine and I won't have her forever. And...we are lovers."

A low growl escaped Alder's throat, but he kept himself reined in. He swayed on his feet and sat back down. I reached over and took his hand. I could tell he didn't know what to say.

David poured whiskey from a crystal decanter into three glasses, and we drank them down. "This is why I've been avoiding you. I genuinely don't understand. Willa is your mate. I know this. Everyone knows this."

Alder leaned back into the leather wingback. "To be honest, I'm not jealous. *I should be. Fuck.* Willa is magic embodied. She is the most incredible creature to walk the earth. I won't even try to explain the power she holds."

Tears escaped my eyes and ran down my face. Emotions I had been holding inside spilled forth. Alder noticed and wiped a damp trail from my cheek, and I couldn't keep a huge smile from forming. "She *is* magical. I miss her."

I looked at David and saw a sadness in his glowing eyes. "I'm not jealous either. Willa is ours, but maybe you need her. Even if it's only for a short while." I sniffled and turned to Alder, a little embarrassed that I cried. "*I* need her. Here. *Please*," I begged.

Alder stood again and pulled me to my feet and into his arms. "I know. I need her too. I'll call her before dawn."

David spoke quietly. "Thank you both for not ending me before you heard me out. I'm sorry for not telling you before you arrived. I didn't know how. This has weighed on me all week. I'm ready to rest. Shall we go home?"

WILLA

When I woke up, it was still dark outside. I wasn't sure how long I had been asleep and expected it to be around midnight. I slept with no dreams. Much to my surprise, it was already 4 am. I craved coffee and my bladder cramped, so I got up.

I sniffed the coffee grounds before closing the lid of the coffee maker. Ahh, heaven. My phone rang and my heart fluttered seeing the words MY VAMPIRE light up the screen.

"Well, good morning."

Alder purred. "Mmm, good morning to you, darling. You sound like you were already awake."

"I was. I'm impatiently waiting on this coffee to brew, but my mood just improved hearing your voice. How's Micah? I miss you both terribly."

"He's in the shower. We went to Lust tonight. I'm so proud of him. Micah has incredible restraint and control when feeding. He has a gentle way about him that makes his training easy. I'm thinking...Harris could bring you and Trace over soon. Like...the day after tomorrow?"

"Oh my gosh, yes! Yeah, I'd love that. I need to see you two. Damn, I miss you." I sighed hard. David crossed my mind. Traveling to London in two days meant I would also be meeting him, and things could get very complicated. "Alder?"

"Yes?"

I had to think. I wasn't sure what to say.

"Willa, whatever is on your mind, please, talk to me."

"It's about David Kingswood. I...he's been in my dreams ever since you and Micah left for London. I don't know why or...what any of this means. To me. To you and Micah. To David..."

26

"Wait. Willa, David told me tonight. He told me and Micah and I want you to know it's okay. You're my mate. I know that for certain."

"Of course I am. Forever." I wished Alder was standing in front of me. I would have tackled him. "So, I guess I'll be meeting David soon, but I want to see you and Micah first. Alone."

"Oh, here he is now."

"Willa! Holy shit, I miss you woman! God, the things I'm going to do to you."

I laughed and I heard Alder laughing too. "I love you and Alder so much. I can't wait to see you. I hear you've been behaving yourself. I'm so happy. Another week without you would have been tough."

I heard him whisper to Alder, then return to me. "I, uh, asked him to let me talk to you in private. He's jumping in the shower."

"Why? What's up? Is something wrong?"

"No. Not at all. I just...Alder and I spent some time together tonight and let me just say, he is talented." I laughed hard and he continued. "That mouth of his is really something."

"Well, I'm glad *someone* is getting some. I'm like a dog without a bone over here. Pun very much intended."

Micah moaned. "Oh, Willa, I want to fuck you so bad. I mean I'm constantly hard for you and you're on another continent. Having you and Alder both is going to be like heaven, I swear."

"I'm the lucky one. I heard you had a talk with David Kingswood."

Micah was silent for a few moments. "We did. Have you dreamed of him too?"

"I have. Only since you've been gone, though. It's confusing, but to be honest, I have a peace about it now that it isn't a secret."

"Well, I think David's been dreaming about you for a long time. His eyes are sad. I think he fights demons he keeps to himself. When he spoke of you, the tone of his voice changed. You may be able to reach him in a way no one else can. He said you soothe him."

It was comforting to know this wasn't only about sex or feeding from me. "Thank you for telling me. I hope the next two days fly by. You and Alder probably need to get some rest. And I need to ingest this huge mug of coffee ASAP."

"Yes. I know how you can be without it. I love you, Willa."

"I love you."

Alder's smooth voice returned. "Have a great day, darling. I'll text you after dusk."

WILLA

Trace came into the kitchen sniffing the air. "Mmm, blessed bean juice."

"Yasss," I laughed. "I have great news. We're leaving for London the day after tomorrow!"

"Seriously? It will take us two days to pack. How exciting. You're looking radiant. Feel better?"

"Oh, yes. It's hard to explain, but I know you understand. The energy I've had lately has been stale and damp. Those are the best words I can come up with. Talking to Alder and Micah filtered it out. Now I'm overflowing with anticipation. I'll do some grounding before my shower with Hiddles."

Trace laughed then eyed me over the steam rising from her cup. "I know you're keeping something from me. Not necessarily something bad, but when are you going to tell me?"

I couldn't help but grin because if I was being honest with myself, the thought of meeting David Kingswood thrilled me. "Let's sit."

"Oh, this is going to be good."

"I've had two dreams about David Kingswood. I thought I

was naked in a bed with Alder in one." I clicked my tongue. "Not Alder."

Trace's eyes were wide. "Oh, fuck. And the other one?"

"Nothing too scandalous. We were in David's office discussing our...whatever it is. We seemed close. I mean, emotionally. Alder and Micah know. Apparently, David's been having dreams about me too. For a while."

"Willa, in a short time you've gone from having zero romantic relationships to having a harem."

"Ha! No lies detected. It's all so crazy. There's no anger or jealousy. Only wonder about what the future holds."

"We should definitely do a clarity spell tonight."

WE STOOD across from each other at my recently unused fortune telling table. Trace lit a yellow candle. "Oh, wait." She went to the window and opened it. "Okay." She handed me the spell to be cast, then lit a sage smudge stick and held it while I spoke.

I call upon the power of air
To clear the mind of confusion
To focus my thinking
And blow away the clutter
That keeps me from making good choices
Blow in the winds of clarity
And help me to think rationally and clearly
So mote it be

I blew out the candle, and she wafted the extra smoke out of the window before closing it. "I'm not a fan of the smell of this sage. I need to find an alternative. I'm sure Marita has something exquisite. I want her Dragon's Blood sage."

"I want so many things from the boutique," I joked.

Seven

MICAH

I could hardly rest during the day. My body vibrated in anticipation of seeing Willa. I had sent way too many sappy texts to her every time I tossed and turned. And every time, Alder grumbled and mumbled for me to be still and put my phone down.

David was waiting for us in the kitchen when we got up at sundown. "Good evening, gentlemen." He was at ease with us now that the air had been cleared between us. He poured fresh warm blood from a carafe into tea cups.

I smelled it before taking a sip. "Well, this is a first. Willa would make some cheesy joke about this if she was here."

David smiled. "I wanted to discuss her arrival. The last thing I want is for Willa to be uncomfortable. I'm thinking she and I could have something like a first date, perhaps? It might take the pressure off of being together right away. There's a gala tomorrow night to kick off fashion week. I would like Willa to be my date."

I audibly scoffed at first, then adjusted my tone. No one was seeing Willa before me. I had been taken away from her as soon as we had been reunited. "I'm sorry, but..."

Alder stopped me. "Micah. Hold on. You will be meeting Harris at the airport. I've arranged for you and Willa to spend a few hours together at my studio flat. I'm sure the gala starts later. No need to worry."

I looked at David. "I apologize. I'm just really amped up. I agree, a public place will be best. I trust you are more than capable of taking care of her?"

David nodded. "Indeed. I would die to protect her," he stated very seriously. I believed him. "And I have reserved you, Alder, Harris, and Trace a table as well."

"Okay. That's settled then, I guess." I rubbed my stomach. "I'm still hungry."

Alder patted me on the back. "Tonight we are going out to Camden. There's always a good bit of live music. I know you like that. This will be part of your training. Mingling with humans while your hunger builds isn't easy."

"What if I lose control or something?"

"I'm bringing Aleksandra. If you just can't help yourself, she will be there to…fill your need, if you will."

"Out in public? I'm just supposed to feed from her?"

Alder came close, standing almost nose to nose with me. "Let me teach you a vampire trick." One hand cupped the back of my head and fisted in my wavy hair. The other went around my waist. He pressed our bodies together, then kissed me. He trailed his kisses along my jaw and settled on my neck where he licked across my tingling skin. I groaned and my cock swelled. He nuzzled his nose to my earlobe. "See? A little feeding looks a lot like making out in a dark corner," he whispered into my ear.

I tightened my arms around him. "Maybe you should show me one more time, so I won't forget." I found his mouth and my tongue tasted the salt from my own neck. Then I remembered David was still in the room and I leaned back.

He watched us. Alder cleared his throat and stepped out of my arms. "Why don't we head out, Micah? David is going to the club."

"Mmm, yes. I need to release a little tension myself," David hummed.

I imagined the gorgeous vampire acting out some of his own fantasies in one of the back rooms down the dark hall of his club.

ALEKSANDRA MET us at The Underworld. It was an alternative rock club nestled underground below a pub called The Worlds End. I was used to this kind of crowd, drinking out of sweating beer bottles and bouncing to the beat of live music, but this time it definitely felt different. The bass pounded in my chest. I could see the features of the faces clearly even in the dim lighting. The British accents mumbling into women's ears of guys trying to get laid. And the smells. Cheap perfume and cigarette smoke mixed with the most potent scent. Blood. I winced at the stabbing sensation that seemed like it branched out in a lightning pattern through my abs. I sucked in a quick breath. My fangs threatened to descend, and I looked back at Alder who was behind me. He put a hand on my shoulder and spoke into my ear. "Easy. Your eyes are glowing. Beautiful." He gave me a quick peck on the lips. "Try to think about the music. It sounds like your type."

"My type? What's wrong with it? What do you like?"

Aleksandra hopped up on a stool at a small high-top table and we joined her. Alder answered my inquiry. "Classical, jazz, 80s, I even enjoy top 40 hits. Maybe I can learn to like this grungy stuff."

I laughed. "Grungy. Yes, I'll get you to like it. And it's called alternative now. What about you, Aleksandra? What are you into?"

She flagged down a cocktail waiter. "Oh, um, The Strokes, Coldplay, Psychedelic Furs..."

Alder laid five twenty-pound bills on the table and shoved it towards the waiter. "Whatever they want." Aleksandra's eyes widened. "How much are we drinking tonight? Are you trying not to think about your sweet human coming to Lust? You know Mr. Kingswood loves to have a little fun with new guests."

I sat up straight. "What? What do you mean?"

She looked at Alder. "He doesn't know?"

Alder shook his head. "It won't be like that with our Willa. She's different. She's our mate and David is very aware."

I pressed Alder. "What are you not telling me about David?"

The waiter placed frosted bottles on the table and Alder drank almost the whole thing. Aleksandra smirked as she sipped hers. She looked amused at our conversation. I was becoming more and more territorial, and Willa wasn't even here yet.

Alder finally answered, "David is a Dom."

Of course, I knew what a Dom was, but I tried to work out in my head what that meant for Willa. Domination took many different forms. Some simply controlled their subjects during sexual play. Sometimes subs were treated like slaves. At the extreme end, Doms could be outright abusive. I searched Alder's eyes. He knew my thoughts.

"Don't worry. I'm going to talk to him before the gala while you and Willa are at my flat."

My knee nervously bounced up and down. Aleksandra put a hand on it to calm me. "Micah, Alder would never let Mr. Kingswood hurt her. I've never seen him hurt anyone."

"You mean, you've *watched*?"

She smiled slyly. "Well, yes. Anyone can watch if you're in the right room."

Suddenly I was in a terrible mood, and I was hungry. "I guess I missed *that* part of Lust. Damn." Another pain shot through me, and I almost doubled over. Alder pointed to the restrooms. "Why don't you and Aleksandra visit the loo?"

Eight

WILLA

Alder had texted telling me to bring a couple of formal dresses. I zipped up the largest luggage I could find. I probably overpacked, but I wasn't sure what all I would need for London. I didn't really know how long we were staying either. Trace walked in as I pushed the heavy wheeled bag towards my door.

"Hi. I'm all packed too. I can't believe we get to go to London during fashion week. It's going to be amazing. Want to go to Boutique du Vampyre with me? I called Marita. She has the Dragon's Blood sage I want and I'm going to get a few other things for the trip."

"Yeah, sounds good. Can we grab brunch at the Café?"

Trace's eyes lit up. "Oh yes, it's been too long since I've had a bloody mary."

"Same." My nerves could use a little relaxing.

BOUTIQUE DU VAMPYRE was one of my favorite places on the planet. Walking in the door calmed me and the scents of fortune candles saturated my senses. Marita came from around the counter for hugs. She had become our good friend and witchy advisor. A kindred spirit who understood much of the world we now lived in.

She hugged Trace, then me. "Willa, I haven't seen you in weeks."

"I know. Life has been...well, you know."

She smiled. "I do. And how is Micah? Is the change going well for him? It can be a struggle at first."

"Alder took him to London. They are there now, and Harris is going to fly us over tonight. Alder said Micah's training has been easier than expected. I'm so thankful."

"He's always been a kind man. I love it when you bring him into the shop. I hope he will be back."

"I'm sure. All of this intrigues him. And he's seen it work first hand."

Trace dumped an armful of items onto the counter. I laughed a little. She shrugged. "We'll be prepared for anything."

Marita laughed too. "If you need anything, I'm a phone call away. And if things get wild, I love London. I wouldn't be opposed to jumping on a quick flight."

"Oh, I have you on speed dial," Trace joked.

Marita covered Trace's hand with hers. "I'm being light-hearted, but seriously...enjoy your time, but be wary. Spirit guides will be with you both. I feel something, or *someone*, blocking me from any clear insight surrounding the coming days. The unknown can be exhilarating. It can also bring darkness. Trust your vampires to protect you."

Marita pulled an amulet from her pocket and placed it in my palm. I turned it over, rubbing across the etched symbol.

"A septagram. The seven-pointed star serves long-life and protection," she explained then paused and searched my eyes. I closed them and she took my hand. I let my energy flow into her fingers. "The septagram consists of the union of four. I believe there is a fourth who will be important on your journey through life. And your presence just might save theirs. Be on your guard, but...let the right one in, Willa."

David's face flashed in my mind. I think Marita saw it too. I slowly opened my eyes, and she released my hand after giving it a knowing squeeze. Trace broke the moment of silence. "Can we do a small spell? The power of three can strengthen its magic."

Marita lit a white candle and she and Trace stacked hands on top of mine holding the amulet. Trace recited the words.

Day and night, safe and sound
We are protected by Divine Light

Marita didn't snuff out the candle. She stuck it in a brass candlestick holder next to the cash register. "It is important to let the wick burn out on its own."

I hugged her tight. "Thank you. We will be in touch."

"Safe travels, my friends."

Nine

MICAH

Alder nudged me in the back. "Micahhhh. Please, be still. You need rest," he moaned and pleaded. "And so do I."

I flipped over and wrapped him up in my embrace. I kissed his forehead and rubbed my nose to his. "I'm trying. I promise."

He smiled, eyes still closed. "I know, but we only have a couple more hours to go."

I closed my eyes and imagined Willa laying between our bodies where she belonged. Soon.

NEVER IN MY LIFE, had I ever thought I would meet the famous male model David Kingswood, and I certainly never imagined seeing him naked. Yet here he was. Walking around his kitchen looking like he was fresh out of the shower. His perfect body on full display.

Alder whispered into my ear, "He has a habit of doing this. Don't think a thing about it."

Right, I thought. David served up fresh blood in tea cups again. I rather liked it all fancy like this. He set the carafe in front of me. "The rest is for you. You should have your fill before meeting with Willa."

Alder nodded. "There will be more at the flat, in case you feel the slightest inkling of pain. You will have about two hours before a car will arrive for Willa and I'll pick you up. Harris and Trace will be along, too."

I put my hand over his. "Thank you for giving us time."

He winked and leaned in close. "I want you to enjoy yourselves. The more pleasure, the better. Remind Willa who she belongs to before her night out on the town."

I knew exactly what he meant, and I would be happy to oblige. I'm sure David heard us. He was smiling from ear to ear before he sauntered out of the room in his birthday suit.

WILLA

There are natural supplements that work very well for sleep, but I didn't take any chances. One Benadryl had me out for a good six hours on the flight to London. The reclining seats aboard the Invictus were perfectly comfortable for the extra-long nap. The last two hours, however, went painfully slow, and I could barely sit still in my seat.

Pent up sexual energy circled what felt like my entire nervous system as the jet touched down. Spiritual and emotional energy mixed in as well, which made me feel high. My soul urgently desired its mates. I slid down the covering over one window to see two fully blacked out SUVs parked near our private runway and a couple of men loaded our luggage into one of them.

As the airstair door lowered, I spied Micah stepping out of one of the vehicles. His eyes glowed and I practically ran down the steps and flung myself into his arms. He swung me around and didn't let go. Finally, I thought. "Yes, finally," he said wistfully. "I love you. I love you *so* much," he added. He leaned back just a little. "Are you sure you're okay with this? I mean, not seeing Alder for a little while?"

I kissed him. My tongue assaulted his. The kiss was desperate. "I've needed this for so long. I need *you*. I can't get you alone fast enough." He smiled again and picked me up like a new bride to carry me to the SUV. I yelled a goodbye to Trace and Harris over Micah's shoulder.

A privacy screen blocked the driver's view of us in the back and there was ample room even with Micah's long legs, so I straddled his lap and looked at his face.

The light in his eyes brightened. "I've missed you. You are *so beautiful.*"

I ran my hands through his wavy blond hair. His wide palms firmly pushed my hips down, pressing me against his hard on. He smiled and ran his tongue over his fangs. I kissed him and let my tongue have a feel too. The sharp points that I knew would soon be pricking my skin turned me on more than I already was. He gripped my bottom with long fingers that I wanted between my legs. Then he slid his hand down my yoga pants to the place I yearned for it to go, and a whimper escaped my throat. My ringing phone jolted me out of the moment, but Micah kept rubbing my clit with his thumb.

"Seriously," I huffed. "Right now?"

Micah kept kissing my neck and whispered against my skin. "You better see who it is. What if it's Alder?"

He still didn't stop pleasuring me and I was about to come. I grabbed my phone from my purse to see an unknown number from the UK. "I don't know who it is."

"Just answer it. I don't mind."

Micah enjoyed teasing me. I breathlessly answered. "H...Hello?"

"Ms. Deberry, good evening. This is David."

Yes, I knew who it was. I recognized his voice from my

dreams. I tried my best to sound casual, but I was dangerously close to crying out as an orgasm hit. I looked at Micah who hummed wickedly. I bit into my lip hard. I covered the phone while I panted, then spoke.

"Mr. Kingswood, hi. How are you?" God, I sounded like a prude.

He laughed. "Please, call me David. I know we already have plans decided, but I wanted to do this right and formally ask you out on a date."

Such a gentleman. "Oh, yes. That's so nice. Of course. I'm looking forward to it. And to meeting you." Micah pulled my t-shirt over the top of my breasts and slid the lace down to do as he pleased. He tongued a nipple and I mouthed *oh god, don't stop*.

David's voice brought me back. "And I you, dear Willa. A car will pick you up from Alder's flat at 7:30. See you soon."

"Sounds perfect. Thank you." I hung up and threw the phone down in the car seat. "Oh, Micah, you devil! You're evil...and I love it."

He stopped from going further and biting me.

"Wait. I want to wait to taste you. Not here in the car."

I sighed and wanted to tease him back. I whispered into his ear, "Alright, but as soon as we get into the flat, I want you to drink me while you fuck me."

"Holy shit, Willa. I've been waiting for this." He gently put my bra and shirt back in place as we pulled up to the curb in front of a red brick building.

The inside of the studio flat was immaculately clean. The décor was very much in contrast to Alder's all-gray lair in New Orleans. The walls were red and emerald green velvet covered the couch and bed. A note from Alder sat on the counter of a kitchenette.

There is food and fresh blood in the fridge if you get hungry. Have fun, lovers.

After Micah hung my formal dress on the bathroom door

along with his tuxedo, I immediately began taking off his clothes. "I need you. Now."

I shoved him down to his back on the bed and quickly shed my clothes. His cock was long, hard, and ready for me. Sharp fangs and glowing eyes beckoned me to take what I needed. I climbed on top of him, and he ran his hands up my arms.

"Willa, I love you. You are *so* beautiful." My hair fell across his shoulders when I leaned down to kiss his lips. He breathed in my scent. "Mmm, you smell amazing."

"I love you, too." I moaned. "Fuck me, Micah."

As soon as I said it, he flipped me over on my stomach and slammed his cock all the way inside me from behind. It was rough and fast, and I loved it. I gasped and a wave of energy seemed to explode in the center of my chest. His hips and thighs hit the back of my ass over and over. I sent the energy down to where our bodies were joined, and he roared when he felt the vibrations. "*Fuck!*" He slowed the pace as the sensation throbbed around his cock. "You are magic, Willa. Let me taste you."

He stayed inside me, but the thrusts were slow and steady as he bent down, pressing his chest against my back. He wrapped one hand around my throat, and he moved my hair out of the way with the other. His tongue was warm when he licked the sensitive place behind my ear. The place where he would have his first taste of me.

"Take it, Micah. Please."

He smelled my skin again before sinking in his fangs. My pelvis rolled in response and my second orgasm of the night clenched around Micah as he came at the same time. I loved feeling his cock pulsating inside me and his mouth latched onto my neck. He let go of my throat and sweetly ran his hand down my spine then seductively squeezed my ass as he retracted his fangs and licked the wound. I didn't move, enjoying the moment.

When he slid out of me, I whined playfully. "I don't want you to move."

He laughed and turned me over. "I wanna hold you."

I reached out to pull him down and I laid on his chest. I nuzzled and kissed his collarbone. His arms held me so tight.

"I hope David doesn't mind seeing the bite mark on your beautiful neck."

"Mmm, he'll just have to deal with it, won't he? It will be faint in a little while." I raised up to look into his eyes. "I never knew love could feel like this before I met Alder, and before I knew you and I had a chance to be...something great. I never wanted sex so much either."

Micah laughed. "Me either. On both accounts." He got serious. "And if David Kingswood needs a little bit of that love, I'm okay with it. I want you to know I'm not jealous, just a little territorial."

He smirked and I gave him a peck on the lips. "I'm not sure what he needs yet, but I wouldn't give him any part of myself if you and Alder weren't okay with it. Never ever. I'm yours." I nibbled his bottom lip. "Are you still hungry? I'll grab you some blood."

"Okay. Get a water. You should hydrate." I hopped up and Micah slapped my ass hard. I yelped and jumped off the bed. "Yes, sir."

Ten

WILLA

I stepped into my red satin dress and stood in front of a full-length mirror. "Hey, can you zip me?" I asked over my shoulder. Micah came behind me and rubbed his knuckles up my spine, sending tingles through my body before slowly dragging the zipper to the top. I let my head fall back onto his shoulder and he inched closer to kiss the wound again. His lips tickled my skin when he spoke. "Have fun tonight. I know you're nervous. Alder and I will be close by if you need us."

I turned in his arms. "I know. I'm glad it was David's idea that you also attend. It puts me more at ease. You better get your tux on."

The intercom speaker on the wall buzzed. "Ms. Deberry, a car has arrived for you," the man working the lobby desk of the building stated.

I went to push the button. "I'm on my way out. Thank you."

I kissed Micah one more time before saying goodbye.

I DIDN'T EXPECT to see a beautiful man dressed in a black suit who wasn't David Kingswood leaning against the car, waiting for me. He reminded me of Clark Kent. Kind of nerdy but handsome and built like a brick wall. He pushed off of the door and opened it, intently watching every move I made. I paused to look back into his eyes.

He nodded his head. "Ms. Deberry, I presume? Good evening. Mr. Kingswood will be meeting you at the gala."

I smiled. "And you are?"

He looked surprised that I asked and cleared his throat. "Well, I'm William...I...I'm security." Heat burned in his eyes. He didn't hide his attraction toward me.

I smiled again. "It's nice to meet you, William."

His eyebrows lifted as I ducked into the car. He closed the door, sank into the driver's seat, and we were on our way. We didn't exchange any more words until we arrived at Somerset House. He pulled to the curb and handed the keys to the valet before extending a hand to help me out. He tucked my arm around his elbow and escorted me down the red carpet. I couldn't keep my hand from vibrating against his bicep. The excitement had built the entire drive. At least they weren't glowing. William looked down at me with raised eyebrows again. He was unsure of what to do with me and my energy. When we stepped inside, I slid my arm from his and nervously rubbed my palms together.

William touched my elbow. "Are you alright?" His eyes were sincerely concerned.

I took a deep breath. "I will be. I promise. Where's Mr. Kingswood? I think all of this waiting is making me antsy," I laughed.

William placed a hand to my back, and we walked into a huge ballroom, bright, shining, and already packed with gorgeous people. Several vampires were in attendance too. Their eyes gave them away.

William pointed. "He's just over there. I'm sure he has a few interviews to do before he can enjoy himself. It's always the case."

David stood tall and straight, feet shoulder-width apart with his hands in the pockets of an expensive black velvet tux while the clicking cameras captured pics for the gossip columns. It felt good to finally be in the same room with him. I could easily see why he was so successful. He dominated the space. Peace came over me and I patiently waited. As if he sensed me, his warm brown eyes found mine and my heart banged against my chest. The corner of his mouth turned up and he came my way.

David reached us and slapped William on the shoulder. "Thanks for driving, mate." Then he turned his body to me, without making eye contact, seeming a bit stuffy and aloof. "It's such a pleasure to meet you, Willa. Thank you for being my date." He nodded a dismissal to William and started walking away. I looked at William who motioned for me to follow after David. What in the world? I had to walk briskly to catch up. I didn't like it. I must have looked like a puppy trailing her master. David pulled out a chair at a six-foot rectangle, linen covered table where no one else was seated yet. Our place cards sat in front of a big bouquet of red roses. There was a perfect view of the center stage and runway. I sat down as he eased into the chair beside me, and I put my hands in my lap, unsure of how to act. Maybe I was only his arm candy tonight. Oh well, I had been thoroughly sexed up by Micah and was determined to eat lots of gourmet food, drink fine wine, and enjoy myself, even if David didn't. I knew I would get to sleep between Alder and Micah in a few hours and that made me happy.

People kept stopping at our table to speak to David who had yet to talk to me again and hadn't introduced me to any of them, so I waved over a waitress. I took two glasses of bubbly champagne from her tray and thanked her. The first one was emptied immediately. When I slammed it down a little harder than I intended, I got David's attention.

He actually looked at me now. "Willa, is everything okay?"

I huffed, not hiding my irritation. There had been so much energy and too many emotions swirling within me and I couldn't contain them all. "What *is* this?" I whispered. "Why, exactly, am I here?"

David scooted his chair closer and turned to me. His knee touched mine and my mouth went dry. "I apologize. I mean it." Our eyes locked and he licked his lips. "I've been nervous about this night ever since I knew you were coming. I'm happy you agreed to this date, but now I'm rethinking it. Maybe our first meeting shouldn't have been in such a public place, because all I want to do is touch you, Willa."

I grabbed my second glass of champagne and swallowed it in two gulps. Then we both laughed, and the mood lightened considerably. I sighed. "You have a way with words, Mr. Kingswood."

He put an arm around the back of my seat. "Call me David."

"But I haven't heard one single person call you that. Maybe I shouldn't either. Especially here."

He shook his head and smiled. "But I want you to."

"Alright, alright. I will. And...don't ignore me just because you're nervous. I promise I'm all aflutter here."

We laughed again and the alcohol hit me. "Wow, I shouldn't have downed those drinks so fast. I need to eat something."

David's eyes glimmered and I knew he was thinking about tasting my blood, but he stood and pulled me to my feet. "Come on then. Let's get you some hors d'oeuvres and..."

David stopped abruptly when he felt the energy flowing from my hand into his. His face said he wanted to devour me. His voice sounded like silk. "This." He laced our fingers together. "I felt you and your magic in my dreams."

I smiled. "Yes. I know...David."

His eyes closed and contentment washed over his model-perfect features. He took in a deep breath and let it out. "Food. You need food." And with that, a new bond was formed, and we found the fancy appetizer buffet together.

"Do you always give off so much energy?" David asked while I gingerly chose various treats with tiny silver tongs.

"Um, yes, a lot of the time I do. I've learned to ground myself, but I was so wound up traveling all night, finally seeing Micah, and then meeting you, a little was bound to escape."

"Well, I find it fascinating. *You* are so very fascinating, and I can't wait to learn more."

I swooned a bit. "Same here."

After returning to our seats and clearing every morsel off of my fine China plate, Alder entered my mind. Oh my gosh, I hadn't thought about Alder or Micah being here. My eyes darted around looking for them. Maybe they hadn't arrived yet. Harris and Trace were nowhere to be seen either. David brought me out of my thoughts.

"It's about time for the runway show," he said, glancing at his Cartier watch. "I don't miss standing on the catwalk. The chaos backstage and the bundles of nerves all tied up. My first few shows, I threw up beforehand."

I guess I had never thought about how terrifying it could be up on a stage in front of the world. "I bet. The heels alone would have me running away."

He laughed. "Oh, I've seen so many ankles giving way and girls tumbling over the edge. And no one is there to pick you up. You have to dust yourself off and keep going."

The lights dimmed and electronic dance music bumped through the ballroom. David settled back into his seat and placed my hand on his hard thigh, lacing our fingers together again. Sexy brocade corsets paired with skinny velvet cigarette pants were worn by both men and women. Then, short, plaid pleated skirts and suede knee-high boots in all colors brightened the stark white runway. I enjoyed the show, and the way David rubbed his thumb down the middle of my palm. It felt similar to grounding in a way. He calmed me and I concentrated on releasing energy through my feet instead of the heat simmering down below. After about fifteen minutes, David let go of my hand and stood. "I'll be back."

Next were long flowing dresses of silk in black, crimson, and emerald. They were absolutely gorgeous and looked like they could be worn by any shape or size. A tall older woman, who I assumed was a former model, stepped up with a mic. "Thank you for being here this evening. The Midnight Gala has always been an important fundraiser for many charities in London and we thank you for your generous donations and bids in the annual auction. Everything you see here tonight will be up for bidding. Dig deep." Everyone laughed. "And now let's show our admiration for the designer, David Kingswood. Come on, David."

The room full of people stood and clapped as David walked out from backstage, kissed both of the woman's cheeks, and took the microphone.

"Cheers, Amelia. Yes, thank you again for attending. I spent a lot of work, time...and money designing for the show tonight and the new season. I know it's very different from what you've seen from me in the past, but I put my heart and soul into this line and if you love it, raise those bids, mates."

Laughter spread out again and David bowed in thanks before leaving the stage. I felt such pride for him.

When he returned and sat next to me, I grabbed his hand. "Oh my god. I loved everything. Those dresses! And the boots!"

He smiled. "I want to see you in those boots. I think I can get you a pair. I know a guy." He winked.

"I'll take them in blue, please."

"Mmm, yes. My favorite color. And...thank you for your compliments. It means a lot to me coming from you."

"Me? Why? I'm nobody."

His eyes burned. "Willa. Stop. You're everything. One sweet word uttered from your lips gives me wings."

I knew I blushed. I felt the heat on my cheeks. "David, you might want to reserve that opinion of me until after we've spent a little more time together."

He pulled my hand to his mouth and kissed my fingers quickly before putting it back down, away from prying eyes. "I'll treasure every moment. Willa, the time we've spent together in my dreams has felt so real. Do you remember when we were in my office?"

I remembered. I remembered the way his nose felt nuzzled near my ear. "Yes."

David whispered, "It *was* real. You were with me. I don't know how you did it, but you were in my office with me for those fleeting moments."

I nodded. I knew it had been real. I had never admitted it to myself. I didn't know how either. "I mean, I don't know. Astral projection?" I laughed nervously because I knew there was no explanation.

"Whatever it was brought you here and I'm forever thankful."

I squeezed David's hand and he straightened. We would be talking more about this in private, I was sure. His eyes darted up behind me and I heard a familiar voice. My mate.

"Good evening. Are you two getting along?"

I stood and turned to Alder. I wanted to leap into his embrace, but I was here with David, so I refrained, as hard as it was. "Hi. I've missed you." My eyes got misty.

Alder leaned in and kissed both cheeks. "I've missed you, darling."

"Mr. Kingswood has been the perfect gentleman and, oh my gosh, weren't his designs just gorgeous?"

Alder smiled. "Yes. I think you would be lovely in one of David's dresses."

David stood. "Indeed she would. Listen, I need to go see to a few details before the conclusion of the auction. You two should take a twirl around the dancefloor with the others. I know you haven't seen each other for a while."

"If you insist." Alder grinned.

David kissed my cheek as Alder watched before stepping away, and I felt like the center of the universe. I was the sun and the planets, my beautiful vampires revolved around me in perfectly orchestrated chaos.

Alder pulled me close, and we swayed. I placed my hand on

his chest to share my energy. His heart started to beat stronger, and his fingers pressed into my hips. I wanted to take him away, out of the crowd, and let him have his way with me, but that wasn't an option. He knew my thoughts. "Soon. Remember, you're coming home with me tonight."

I scoffed. "Yes, to *David's* home."

"Oh, there's plenty of privacy there. Would you rather go to my flat? I don't care where we are, as long as you are next to me... under me...on top of me..."

I laughed, but my body burned. "Stop it. I'm extremely turned on and can't do a damn thing about it right now." I leaned up on my toes to whisper in his ear, "I'm so wet for you."

I lingered there, my nose skimming along his neck to smell the familiar apple and cedarwood scent I loved so much. Alder growled and leaned back. His eyes were flecked with sensual sparks. His tongue ran over teeth behind his lips, and I knew his fangs had descended.

In a few moments, after they retracted, he smiled mischievously. "Yes, under me will do just fine, darling." He suddenly swung me around and my backside bumped into someone. I startled and turned around to apologize.

"I'm so sorry..."

It was Micah. And he held on to Trace. My heart swelled. "Well, hello, you two." I left Alder's arms and hugged my best friend tightly. "I've missed you."

Trace giggled. We were always giddy around each other. Our energies were soulmates, and I was a better human just being near her.

"I've missed you too."

"Wait. Where's Harris?"

Micah frowned. "He's not feeling well, so he didn't come."

"What?" I turned to Alder. "Vampires get sick?"

He winced. "Not usually. Only when we haven't eaten for a very long time, or..."

"Or what?"

"Or if a witch puts a spell on you," Trace replied in a worried tone. "I think we may have to call Marita."

"Of course, we should."

"We will after the gala. It's only 6 am there, remember. It's okay. Harris isn't too bad for now. He's resting and told us not to worry."

I sighed. "Well, it didn't take long for all of us to be thrown back into some drama, did it?"

Micah grabbed my hand. "Maybe you and Trace could do a little spell later tonight. Couldn't hurt."

I pulled his arm around my shoulders. "That's a great idea." He kissed my forehead. I stepped back when I noticed David making his way over to us and he gently touched my elbow.

"Hi. Sorry about that. I'm free from my responsibilities for the rest of the evening. I'd love to have a dance with you before the party is over."

"Of course. Let's get out there." I looked over my shoulder as he led me away.

"See you all in a bit." Alder winked.

David put one hand on my waist and held the other up for me to hold. I could tell he was being either hesitant or careful with me, so I confidently and securely placed mine in his. I wanted him to know I sincerely trusted him. I circled my energy within myself so he wouldn't get overwhelmed or extremely turned on, which sharing energy had a tendency to do. His eyes already glowed brighter with only a touch. My other hand stayed on his arm since he kept some space between us.

His eyes darted around. "Everyone's watching."

I looked past him, then back to his gaze. "They look like they should be used to all of this. All of these social butterflies."

"Well, I don't bring dates to most functions. I'm a very private person."

"Aren't most vampires private?"

"Even before. Being well recognized comes with a fair share of people wanting to use you for money or fame. Or they take of you physically, not concerned about knowing who you are beneath the grandeur."

I noticed a couple of photographers snapping their cameras. "Are you alright with them?" He knew who I was talking about.

"I am. Not normally, but I think our situation is different. Something has brought us together. You have mates. You aren't staying here, so if everyone thinks we are together, maybe it will appear that I'm off the market and will be left alone. It may just be the perfect arrangement."

I stopped moving with him. "Wait. Is this all you want from me? Am I here as a show for you, so you can obtain your own peace? Because the dreams I have of you are *not* bringing me any fucking peace. If that's all you want, you can hop into someone else's life." I pulled out of his hold and walked away as calmly as I could.

"Wait," I heard him call. I knew he wouldn't run after me because all eyes were still on us.

I didn't need this shit in my life. I belonged to Alder and Micah and I sure as hell didn't need the dreams to continue. I had already formed an emotional and physical attachment to David. It was all too much. I grabbed my clutch from the table and made a beeline to the red exit sign and left the ballroom.

Eleven

MICAH

W illa was mad. I felt it and stood up from our table to search the room. Alder sensed it too. We watched Willa walk out and David headed towards us.

"Go find her," Alder told me. "I'll speak with David."

Within a couple of minutes, I found Willa sitting on a couch in the lobby. I sat next to her and pulled her to my side.

"What's wrong? David is talking to Alder. I know he upset you."

"Oh, he upset me alright. I'm not a pawn. I won't be used for anyone's convenience."

"Willa, I don't think that's what's going on, but if you really feel that way, we'll leave."

She rubbed her temple. "I'm not sure what to think."

"We need to sort it all out at David's house. Not in public. And I'm not leaving your side until you ask me to."

Willa laid her head on my shoulder, and I loved being her protector. I took her hand while we waited for Alder and Trace.

"Do you feel the rug under your feet?"

She nodded.

"Take off your heels. Send the negative energy out while you take some deep breaths." She did and her tension eased.

"You are so good for me," Willa whispered.

"I know," I said with exaggerated confidence, which made her laugh.

It wasn't long until Alder and Trace located us, and David was with them. Willa rolled her eyes and didn't acknowledge him. He knew better than to address her, so Alder spoke.

"We should go. David and I will take his car. We'll see you soon," he stated.

"Fine with me," Willa replied coldly. I shook my head at the others because I knew she had put up a wall that would take a wrecking ball to get through.

TRACE and I didn't push her during the car ride home. I sensed she expelled negative energy with every exhale of breath as she stared out the window, and when we entered the kitchen, Alder and David were there sipping teacups of warm blood. I went straight for the cabinet and took out a large coffee mug. Alder poured it to the brim. He knew I was starving. Willa ignored David.

"Is Trace with Harris?" she asked Alder.

"Yes."

"And he's still the same? Not any worse?"

"No."

"Well, then I'm going to bed. Which room are we in?" she asked me.

David finally spoke. "Willa, can we talk in my office for a few minutes first?"

"Not now," she answered shortly and looked at me, waiting

for me to show her to our room. I took the mug with me and hastily led her down the hall. I wanted to stay on her good side.

We went into the room, and she threw her clutch on the desk, then went into the en suite.

I leaned my forehead on the door she had closed behind her. "Your things have already been put in their places. There's a robe for you hanging on the door."

"I see. Relax, Micah. I'm okay. Drink your blood. I'll be out in a minute."

I heard the sink turn on and Alder came in. "She alright?"

"She will be."

He undressed down to his boxer briefs, so I did the same. When Willa came out, she smiled at us, but looked tired. She went to Alder and mumbled into his chest when he wrapped his arms tightly around her. "I missed you." Then she sweetly placed kisses along his collarbone. His mouth found hers and I watched the most passionate kiss I had ever seen. One arm wound around her waist. He held the back of her head with the other hand and twisted his fist in her hair. Her body arched into him. Willa shed the robe and pulled him down on the bed. My fangs descended and my cock got hard. Alder's long, beautiful body covered hers and he grinded against her, just where she wanted. She panted and moaned as he alternated between kissing her lips and sucking on her neck. Her legs latched around his hips to press even closer, and her fingers pushed his underwear down.

"I want you inside me."

Alder sank into her, and she tried not to cry out. He murmured into her ear while he pumped in and out, "I love you. I've missed you so much, darling. You feel so good." Willa dug her red nails into his back. He slowed his pace and licked her neck.

"Can I take what's mine?" he growled.

"Fuck yes. Please. Bite me, Alder. Take me."

My cock throbbed in the hand I had been rubbing it with and when he bit down to taste our mate, I came into my palm. Now, I panted watching his lips against Willa's skin, drawing from her magic. It reminded me of what he did to me at Lust, and I wanted to be closer to them but wasn't sure if I should. I quickly grabbed a towel from the bathroom and wiped my hand.

Then I heard Willa call my name, "Micah."

I gingerly crawled next to them onto the bed as Alder found release. He clicked his tongue and groaned in satisfaction. He lifted his head from her to look at me with burning brown eyes. Blood dripped from fangs and trickled from his lips, and his mouth curved into a wide wicked grin. I reached out a finger to wipe some from his bottom lip and enjoyed the sample.

"Have some more," he encouraged and grabbed the back of my head to pull me into a kiss. Willa made a contented hum. She reached up and touched my cheek. Alder and I looked down at her and she sighed.

"I love seeing you two together."

Alder looked back to me. "Do you need anything?"

I knew what he meant. "No, I'm all good. Everything is perfect."

I sat back on my heels as Alder slid out of Willa. She turned over and pushed me down. I adjusted so she could scoot up and lay her head on my chest. Alder smiled again and went to clean up. Willa traced the v-line of my hip and I played with her hair.

We stayed there in happy silence until Alder returned.

"Are you tired, darling? It's 2 am. We should let you sleep."

She stretched and sat up. "No," she whined. "I'll sleep with you two at dawn. I need to get used to it anyway. I just want us to be together."

Alder hopped in on her other side and she giggled. "Yes, my mates."

I saw David flash through her thoughts, and I felt that protective feeling creep up. "Alder, I want to talk to David before he speaks with Willa again."

Alder's eyes narrowed. I read his mind. He wondered what my angle was. He was very aware of my newness to being a vampire and didn't want me to lose control if I got angry.

"Alright, reemphasizing your claim on Willa is a good thing, but go easy. David is just as confused over everything as we are. There are a lot of emotions and thoughts on his mind. And unanswered questions."

"So, he's not just using me?" Willa asked.

"No, I honestly don't think so."

"Well, I'll talk to him later. You know, it's really unfair that *I* can't read everyone's mind," she joked.

I almost choked at the thought. "You *do not* need to read my mind. You'd send me to horny jail for life."

"Oh my god," she laughed. "You'd never survive. Wait. Yes, you would. You're a vampire."

"I'd write to you," Alder chimed in.

"Gee thanks," I laughed. "But I've thought about you that way long before becoming a vampire," I told Willa.

"And I had no idea. Alder, would that have changed the way you felt if Micah and I had acted on our mutual attraction? Would I still have been your fated mate?"

Alder caressed her face and touched his fingers to her lips, and she kissed the tips. "The past never dictates fate. You are meant to be mine and I would have simply claimed you as a couple. Especially since it's worked out anyway. This," he took our hands, "is fate."

Willa's hands glowed. I had gotten used to it. I loved it. I think I needed her energy to thrive. I needed her heart and soul to keep me going. She laced her fingers with ours.

"So, what exactly are you going to say to David?" she implored.

"I need to know the truth, see the look in his eyes, when he says he is sincere and genuine about his feelings for you."

Alder squeezed my hand. I squeezed it back. *And* I'm going to threaten his immortal life if anything happens to you while you're in his keep," I promised Willa.

"Well, he's got to convince me first," she stated. "And before I can move forward with any of that, Trace and I have to figure out this situation with Harris. Surely Marita can help."

"I'm sure she can," Alder insisted. "The Kingswood clutch is aware that there may be an ill-natured witch around."

Our discussion was interrupted when Willa's stomach growled. She raised her brows. "What? I'm hungry. It's like 2 am and I only had an enormous plate of little, tiny, itty bitty bites of food. I mean, it was delicious, and piled high, but still. And I swear I smell Trace's pancakes."

Alder got up and handed her a robe then put his boxer briefs back on. "Let's go to the kitchen. You do, indeed, smell Trace's pancakes."

I leapt up so fast. "I may not require a lot of food, but I do love her pancakes."

Twelve

WILLA

O h, of course. Great. David sat at the island. He licked syrup from a long index finger then his thumb. I thought about him licking my...his eyes cut to mine, and I quickly looked away. *Shit!* He read my mind.

Harris stood next to Trace at the cooktop. His eyes had dark circles underneath. I went to him and hugged him tight. "Hi. I heard you aren't feeling well."

"Oh, I'll be fine."

Trace handed me a plate. "I called Marita. She's coming to London. I knew she would. She gave me a couple of spells to try."

David spoke up. "Can I watch you do your spells? I've never been around witches much. And definitely not when they are spell casting."

"Yes. The more good intention in the room, the better." Trace smiled.

"Maybe we should cast a trust spell, so a certain someone will talk to me," David directed at me.

I huffed. "Okay. Your office. Now."

"But...I need to talk to David before..." Micah exclaimed.

I cut him off. "It's fine."

I walked down the hall, and David followed me. He came in behind me and shut the door, but stood, waiting for me to speak. It irked me that he just stared.

"Ugh! Sit down or something," I barked.

He had a heated look in his eyes and obeyed, sitting on a leather couch beside a tall bookcase filled with antique books. I could smell them. I could also smell David. Sweet pipe tobacco like Trace's grandmother used to smoke. I loved the scent. It comforted me. He could tell I liked it. He leaned back and sat with his long legs spread. He looked divine and I wanted to sit in his lap.

"Willa, would you sit next to me? Please."

I pulled my robe tighter and sat closer than I should have. "You have a lot of making up to do, you know?"

That made him laugh. "Oh, Willa, you don't know the lengths I would go to to make it up to you. To...please you."

I looked at him. He held out a hand. "May I?"

I put my hand in his and felt peaceful energy coursing through him. He closed his eyes for a few moments and intertwined our fingers together. "Willa, I've never been a weak man. I'm so weak for you."

"It's not weakness. It's want," I said softly.

David held my hand to his chest. "It's need. I need you. Crave you. Not for publicity. That was just a thought. Something I said in the moment. This goes so much deeper." He let go of my hand and tucked my hair behind my ear. "Willa, can I kiss you?"

I turned toward him with excitement. "Yes."

He leaned in. His nose skimmed my cheek before soft lips tenderly pressed to mine. The short kiss felt safe and sweet, but inside I felt far from innocent. His mouth stayed barely an inch from mine, and I hungrily took his bottom lip between my teeth and tugged. David's eyes flew open and then he growled. His lips crushed mine this time and we grabbed onto each other. My tongue felt his fangs. I moaned and his hand wrapped around my throat. He pulled back a little.

"You're so beautiful and you taste so good. It's painful for me to not take you right here, right now."

My eyes were wide, and he smiled. "Willa, I won't." He let go of my neck and moved to kneel in front of me. He placed my hand around his throat. "I'm sure you've heard things about me. About what I like. How I like sex."

I nodded, looking down at him as he looked up at me in supplication.

"Having control gives me power. Dominating a lover gets me high. It's my drug, but the thought of you taking control exhilarates me beyond any scenario I could ever imagine."

I felt his Adam's apple rolling under my palm as he talked, and I tightened my hold. I had never truly dominated anything or anyone before, but I was ready to learn. He knew what I was thinking.

"You can do anything, Willa. You can do with me what you desire, but..."

"But what?" I whispered.

"Only in private. And I want a bond. A real bond. I've been all alone. Sure, humans and vampires surround me, but I never let anyone in."

I pulled his chin up further and leaned down close. "I'm here. Let me in," I soothed, and then I kissed him, and I felt the need to protect his heart. The famous, powerful vampire needed to feel real love and I fell for David right there with him on his knees before me. When I ended the kiss, he hugged me around my waist. His head lay on my lap. I ran my hands through his hair and let positive energy pulse along his scalp. He grunted contentedly. I didn't make a move to get up until he raised his head and sighed. I took his hands and pulled him to his feet, and he lifted me to mine.

David placed a warm palm to my cheek. "I should get you back to your mates."

When he started to go open the door, I grabbed his wrist. "Wait. Do you get time off? I mean, I know you're the boss, but will you spend a night with me? Alone. Soon."

David's eyes burned brightly. He pushed my hair behind my shoulders and traced a finger down the side of my neck. "We will rest today, and tonight...we will bond."

A thrill ran through me, and I kissed his cheek before we left his office.

THE KITCHEN WAS empty when I walked through the quiet house. Back in our room, Alder sat at the desk, working on his laptop, and Micah flipped through a magazine in bed. They both looked concerned when I walked in. I went to Alder and sat in his lap. He placed a few kisses on my neck.

"I smell David on your skin," he said.

He sounded turned on, which made me tingle all over.

"Does that bother you?"

Fangs pricked my neck and my eyes just about rolled into the back of my head with pleasure. He only took a little, as if he was making the statement that I belonged to him, then he licked the wound.

"No, it doesn't in the least. As long as you are okay and you return to *me*, everything is as it should be."

I put my head on Alder's shoulder with my nose tucked under his chin. "Always. I'm yours." I nuzzled into him and then looked at Micah. "And yours too, I guess," I joked.

Micah kept looking at the magazine. "Damn straight, you are."

Thirteen

TRACE

Sleeping during the day felt strange, but I stuffed Willa's and my pillow with poppy seeds, and it helped tremendously. That is, until Harris groaned a few times and woke me up. I couldn't make out what he said, but I laid my hand on his forehead and it was freezing. Vampires are cooler than humans, but not that cold. And it didn't seem to register I was there or that I had touched him. I looked at my phone to see the time. 4:35 am. It would be another thirty minutes or so before I could wake the others. I had to wait until the sun was below the horizon, so I grabbed the flannel throw from the ottoman and formed it around Harris' face, covering his neck to keep in as much of what little body heat he had.

I went to the kitchen to make coffee and wait for the others to wake. Marco appeared at dusk. He greeted me with a smile and tied an apron around his waist.

"Tonight, we will dine on a traditional English breakfast. I heard you made your famous pancakes."

I laughed. "Yes. I've never had a traditional English breakfast but saw plenty when I scrolled Pinterest, and it looks delicious."

He moved with grace as he worked. The phrase "Whip up a meal" came to mind.

"I know vampires don't need much human food, but do you get as much pleasure out of eating as Harris does?" I asked.

"Oh, yes. It's much like everything else. Sounds are sharper. Sights are clearer. Touch is electric and taste...feels downright sinful. It's one of my favorite things about vampirism. Experiencing every detail of life on a higher level is sublime."

"Willa would say 'Amazeballs'," I laughed.

"I heard that," Willa called from the hall.

She entered with Alder and Micah following behind and came to hug me. "And my best friend is amazeballs," she joked and kissed my cheek. Then she got serious. "What's going on with Harris?"

"I was waiting for all of you because he isn't good. He is absolutely freezing and he's not waking up. I tried to give him some of my energy before I went to sleep, and there is a block there. Something or someone is blocking my ability to connect."

"Sounds like it's time for a spell," Willa stated.

"I know. Marita should be here in an hour or so. Her presence will only strengthen it."

David sauntered in, nodding to all of us, then he kissed Willa's forehead. I guess they had made up. Alder placed a tea cup of blood in front of him.

"David, can you hear Harris? I haven't since he first fell ill. Whatever is blocking the energy is also blocking our bond," Alder said.

David ran a hand through his hair. "Honestly, I can't tell he's in the house. This has to go deep. I had no idea bonds between vampires could be severed this way."

"Well, I've never heard of it in all my years," Marco said over his shoulder. "But witches can be powerful. I think that's why vampires and witches haven't really mixed on purpose. We are leery of one another. Mr. Kingswood's business partner, Ian, might have some thoughts on all of this going on with Harris. Ian has been around a long time. I'm sure he's at least acquainted with witches."

David clicked his tongue. "I just have to pin him down. He was in Bali the last time we texted. But good thinking, Marco."

"Thank you both," I said. "When Marita arrives, I'm hoping you two will join the rest of us in a little spell casting. There is power in numbers. And I know you said vampires and witches haven't mixed in the past, but this involves all of us, doesn't it?" I was desperate for all the help I could get.

"I am more than willing," Marco said.

"Same here," David added.

Marco dished up hearty portions of food and we all sat to eat at a long, formal table in the adjacent room. After a few minutes, the bell rang at the front door and Marco jumped up to answer it. I followed behind him. Willa did too.

Marita entered with a large, handsome man carrying her luggage. I hugged her neck and Willa patted the man on the forearm.

"William, hi. It's good to see you again."

He blushed at her. "Hello Ms. Deberry. Fancy seeing you too."

Oh lord if Willa added another man to her harem...I laughed to myself.

David had joined us to welcome the new arrivals.

"Thank you for picking up Marita, Will."

"Right, boss. Enjoy your night off." He winked before leaving.

"Marita, this is David Kingswood, lord of the manor," Willa joked.

David laughed and extended his hand. "We can't thank you enough for coming. Let me know of anything I can do to help."

Her eyes scanned David's face, admiring his good looks. "It's a pleasure to meet you. I'm a bit of a fan."

I led Marita to the dining room and Marco served her dinner.

"Oh, thank you. I'm starving. Is Harris still nonverbal?"

Hope filled me knowing Marita was here. "Yes. After we get our fill and you get settled, I'll show you."

WE ALL GATHERED AROUND HARRIS. He silently laid in the bed and breath barely escaped his lungs. Marita took his hand.

"Nothing. I feel no energy within his body. We have to get him a shower and then into a cleansing bath. With Harris in this state, we'll need you, Alder, to help Trace and me hold him for both. And David, will you help Willa and Micah set up an alter? Any type. Willa knows what to do. I'll need matches or a lighter. I couldn't bring them in my luggage. We'll do our casting after Harris is back in bed."

"On it," David said.

"I'll fetch matches," Marco declared with purpose.

Willa and Micah followed them out and I began peeling back the covers from Harris. Marita retrieved Epsom salt and rosemary essential oil from her room. Alder and I had Harris stripped and already into a hot shower. I glanced up from my task of bathing Harris when I heard Alder sniffling.

"He's so cold. I've never seen him like this. It takes me back to the night I went to take care of him during the plague. I had prepared myself...to walk into his home and see him deathly ill. I'm not ready for this. Not now," he cried. "Especially now...that he found you."

I cried with Alder, but we kept washing. I couldn't lose Harris. I wouldn't. "Thank you for saying that. Sometimes I feel like a small powerless human, but Harris makes me feel like a goddess."

Harris was clean and rinsed. We dried him off a little and Alder held him while Marita and I filled up the deep soaking tub and added the Epsom salt and rosemary oil. Marita lit a short white candle and swirled the water in a counter clockwise motion. She recited words:

His body is cleansed
His aura is pure
Negative energy will not endure
His will is his own
His path is clear
Malicious energy is unwelcome here

"Alright. Let's all focus on the flame of the burning candle as we lower Harris down into the water. Visualize the bright white light encompassing his body, evaporating away unwanted energy."

Alder held Harris, submerged except for his face, until the candle burned all the way down. Then we lifted him out and placed him on the bed.

David knocked on the bedroom door. "May we come in?"

I covered Harris' naked body. "Okay."

Willa came in with David. "We are ready when you are," she said quietly. I kissed my vampire's cold lips before leaving his side.

We were gathered, somber yet hopeful. Willa placed a white candle in a holder in the middle of Marita's cauldron and filled it with water so that the candle extended above the rim and above the water.

I spoke. "Visualize a dark spell." I lit the candle. "Now visualize the spell being broken."

Marita recited a spell:

Be gone now and hear my verse
The time is now to break the curse
May it be gone and this hex undone
As quickly as it had begun
So mote it be

I stepped back from the alter to join the others in a circle and felt healing, protecting energy swirling within me.

"Let's join hands," I instructed. "Watch the flame. Circle our combined energy. If you feel any negativity, remove yourself from the room."

Out of the corner of my eye, I saw the glow of Willa's hands, which were holding onto Alder and Micah's. My best friend was far more powerful than any of us realized. I saw David glance over at her in awe.

"Everyone concentrate," I reminded them.

We watched the flame extinguish when it met the water. Marita let go of me and Marco to pick up the cauldron.

"The candle and water must be buried in the earth. Preferably near the front entrance of your home, David," Marita instructed.

"I'll grab a spade," he said.

Fourteen

TRACE

After pouring the cauldron water into the hole and burying the candle with it, Marco served warm blood to the vampires and warm tea to us humans. A calm hung over us and I hugged Marita.

"Thank you so much for dropping everything and coming here." I turned to the others. "And thank you all. I think what we've done tonight will help."

"Now we have to find the evil witch," Willa hissed over the edge of her cup.

"We will," Alder assured her. "David, I trust you'll take care of our Willa tonight while Micah and I meet with our contacts here about what's going on. Trace and Marita are going along too. I want them to use their witchy senses, so to speak."

I about choked on my tea thinking about David taking care of Willa and what that might entail.

"Of course," David answered with a straight face. "I've added extra security around the house as well as the club."

"You're sure I'm not needed?" Willa asked.

"I'm sure, darling." Alder kissed her.

"Well, be careful."

WILLA

Marco had disappeared after the others left. Harris slumbered in his room. I had wandered into the room next to David's office. It was a cozy library. I took in the scent of the books and tried to tamp down the jolts of nervousness that threatened to have me hiding away in my room. David and I were going to be alone, and I was unsure what would come next. Did he have a red room, a sex dungeon?

I jumped at the sound of his voice.

"The only red room here is the little loo next to the sitting room."

I sighed. "It really isn't fair. You, reading my mind. I need a spell to block everyone from my thoughts."

He stood next to me, and I smelled him again.

"Is there a spell for that?"

"I have no idea."

My heart beat faster with David so close. "So, what are we going to do tonight?"

He smiled. "Why don't you get comfortable and meet me back here?"

"How comfortable?"

"Hmm, how about pajamas?"

I laughed a little. "Meet you back here then."

I HAD CALMED myself while I put on my nicest nightgown and silk robe but seeing David standing in the hall now wearing only gray sweatpants and bare feet had me buzzing. His eyes glowed and he held out a hand for me to hold. I took it and he led me to his bedroom. The room from my dreams. I let go of his hand and went to touch the carved stone fireplace. There was no fire burning, except the one inside me.

"Looks familiar," I said quietly.

David moved slowly across the room to a small wet bar and poured wine. I sat on the edge of the bed and tried to clear my mind. He sat next to me and handed me a glass. He lifted his.

"Here's to getting to know each other."

We clinked the glasses together. I took a small sip, then turned it up and finished the rest. David laughed.

"Slow down, Willa. I want you to relax. I only want to be with you tonight. I don't have any expectations."

He took the glasses back to the bar top and returned.

"Can I braid your hair?"

I sat there looking at him, not knowing how to respond.

"I know it sounds silly, but it calms me."

"No. No, it's not silly. It's...sweet. I would love it."

I scooted to the center of the bed and David sat cross-legged behind me. He gently ran his fingers through my hair.

"Do you braid all the girls' hair?" I joked.

"Actually, I learned how to do this at runway shows. It's chaos sometimes. Us guys get a little gel in our hair, change out our slacks or speedos," he laughed, and I felt little tugs as he wound the plaits together. "But it takes much more for the girls. The clothes, makeup and one day we were short on hairdressers, so I was pretty much forced to learn. The funny thing is it helped with my pre-show nerves. I stopped getting sick beforehand and I got quite good at it."

He tugged the finished braid and swung it over my shoulder. I ran my hand over the smooth, tight bumps down to the end where the tip felt like a paintbrush. "I'm impressed. You are a very impressive vampire. What other talents are you hiding?"

"Oh, god," he groaned. "You are begging me to be naughty, aren't you?"

I looked over my shoulder and played innocent. "*Who, me?*"

"Yes, you," he replied in a deep sultry tone. "Let me think... there is something I haven't told anyone today."

"Oh yeah, what?"

"It's my birthday."

I turned around so fast. "David! What? Why didn't you say something?"

He looked shy all of the sudden. "I don't like all of the fuss. And there are so many houseguests. And with everything going on with Harris, I—"

I didn't let him finish. I grabbed his face and gave him a kiss. He looked surprised.

"Well, that was nice."

"You deserve a kiss on your birthday."

David reached out and played with the braid. I took his hand and laced our fingers together. My palm vibrated against his and he hummed. I showed him my other palm and he placed his against it. His eyelids closed and I pushed energy into his hands. He gasped and his breathing escalated.

"Babe, wait." His eyes flew open, and he looked at my glowing hands linked with his. "Wait. My heart."

I pulled back the flow of energy and smiled at him calling me babe.

"Willa, my heart is beating so hard. I haven't felt it beat like that since I was a human."

I smiled. "It's okay. You're fine. It won't hurt you. Energy play can do that to a vampire. I promise you're alright."

His perfectly chiseled chest rose and fell, and he put his hand over his heart. I wanted to touch him there too. He knew it. He took my hand and placed it on his cool skin.

"I'm aware of energy play, but what you do is on another level."

"Did I hear you call me babe?" I joked to lighten the mood. "Because...I liked it."

He showed me a wide smile. "Did I?"

"Mmm hmm. You did," I teased. "Thanks for telling me it's

74

your birthday. I won't say anything to the others if you don't want me to, but you deserve a cake or something."

He shook his head. "Oh, no I don't."

"Uh huh, yes you do. You should be celebrated. I've never been to a vampire birthday party."

David fell back with a belly laugh and rolled onto his stomach, burying his head in a pillow. "You're too nice to me. I don't know how to handle you," he mumbled with his face still covered.

"Are you blushing?" I crawled up over his rock-hard ass and straddled his waist. I poked him in the ribs. "Are you?"

He squirmed and bucked beneath me but didn't throw me off. He could have easily. "Oh, no you didn't, lass. I'm very ticklish. I *hate* being tickled."

"Ahhhh, you shouldn't have said that."

Now, he meant business, afraid I would start tickling him again. He flipped his body over, latched onto my wrists, and sat up so we were nose to nose. My nightgown was pushed up around my waist and his hard on pressed against me through his sweats. He inched closer to kiss me, and I leaned back. I remembered what he told me. He wanted me to take control. David's eyes widened when I kept myself beyond the reach of his lips. I looked down at his grasp on my wrists and back up at his eyes.

"Let go," I said gruffly.

He waited a few seconds then released me and carefully placed his hands on either side of my knees, not touching me. I felt his erection growing. I reached out and pushed up the corner of his top lip to see fangs. "You naughty creature. What am I going to do with you, wild one?" My eyebrows shot up. "Ohhh. Someone told me it's your birthday. I think a spanking is in order." David's jaw dropped.

"You wouldn't..."

I hushed him with my hand firmly over his mouth. "Why yes, I would." I kept my voice sexy and my face stern. I removed my hand, and he licked his lips. I dismounted his lap and got up. David watched my every move.

"Let me ask you something first. A simple yes or no answer will do. Have you dreamed of this? I mean this specific scenario between us."

"No."

"Good. I mean, what's the point if you know everything that will happen?"

I felt powerful and it was glorious. I loosened the braid, which had already begun to unravel, and let my hair fall down my back. David groaned.

"Stand up and come here."

He did as I said. His breathing was heavy, and I knew I made his heart beat fast again. I stepped behind him and ran my hands over his shoulder blades and biceps. He shivered. Then, my index finger slid between his waistband and his skin, and I noticed he wasn't wearing any underwear.

"Are you telling me the truth? Are you sure you haven't dreamed of this before?"

He cleared his throat. "I swear."

I fisted my fingers in his short black hair as best as I could and yanked his head back. "Yes or no."

"Yes, yes!"

I let go and he kept his chin up. His long dark eyelashes blinked up at the ceiling. I returned to the sweats and slowly pushed them down to the floor. His chest heaved. He was beautifully bare before me. I forcefully pushed him toward the bed until his knees touched the mattress.

"Bend over," I ordered. "Lay on the bed with your feet on the floor." He obeyed. His arms extended over his head. The vampire was on display and totally vulnerable to me.

"Have you been spanked before?"

"Never, no! No! No no no no," he quickly corrected himself.

I stifled a laugh. Oh, this was too fun. I scratched my nails over the curve of his ass, and he whimpered. His glutes flexed and he pressed his cock into the bed. I traced my name across his iliac crest. "Mmm, yes. W-i-l-l-a. Now you're mine."

Before the thought completely crossed my mind, I reached back and slapped hard. I didn't want him to expect it.

David clenched his glutes together along with his fists into the comforter. His back and calf muscles were strained. I did it again a little harder and he went up on tiptoes. His chest was still. "Don't...hold...your breath."

"Yes ma'am."

Smack!

I hit harder. David hissed and bit down on the covers.

Smack! Again. *Smack!* And again.

I heard his fangs rip through fabric and his hips flexed against the side of the bed as he came. His heels eased down flat onto the floor and his grip on the comforter relaxed, but he stayed put. My body wanted to flip him over and ride him hard, but I briskly walked out of his room, slamming the door behind me. "Happy Birthday," I called through the door.

I flat out ran down the hall into my own room and locked the door. I felt a rush of adrenaline like I had committed a crime and got away with it.

"Well, what have you been up to young lady?"

I yelped at the sound of Micah's voice and spun around to see him and Alder in the bed, bare-chested and looking like they were waiting for a snack. That snack being me.

"I..." I barely uttered.

Alder patted the small space between them. "Join us?"

I sighed with relief, knowing they didn't really want a rundown of what had happened in David's room. I threw off my robe and ran and jumped into bed with my mates.

Fifteen

WILLA

At dusk, I woke up on Micah's chest with his arm securely around me. I lifted my head to look at his face and he opened one eye.

"It's already evening?"

"Yeah." I yawned.

He kissed my cheek and scooted out from under me.

"You're hungry, aren't you?" I asked.

Micah rubbed his abs. "Very. And I can't take a chance, lying there. Smelling you. Wanting to take a little drink."

I stretched like a cat. "I know. I'm sure Marco has a mug of the red stuff waiting for you."

When we walked down the hall to go to the kitchen, Alder and David were coming out of David's office. David smiled at me with raised eyebrows, and Alder put his arm around my waist.

Alder kissed my forehead. "Good evening, Darling. Sleep well?"

"I did. It's getting a little easier to sleep during the day."

To my surprise, Harris sat with Trace and Marita at the island. He gave us a little wave hello. His appearance wasn't one hundred percent but thank the universe he was awake and aware. Marco handed Alder and Micah their blood and started to get my coffee.

"No, no," I shooed him. "I've got this. You sit down."

He and Alder and Micah went to sit in the dining room, and David came to stand next to me while I emptied two packets of Splenda into my mug. I felt his eyes boring into the side of my face, but I avoided glancing his way and poured the coffee. After I replaced the carafe, he grabbed my wrist.

I thought he was mad at me—mad at the way I left him and ran, but his thumb began rubbing over my knuckles. It made me tingle all over. When I finally turned my eyes up to his, they sparked, and he wore a wide mischievous grin. I couldn't help but smile and giggle a little.

"Happy Birthday," I mouthed, and he made a playfully scolding look at me.

"I can't *believe you*, you minx," he whispered.

I gaped at him and whispered back, "Minx? *Me?*"

We turned around and the others were watching us flirt. Even Marco, Alder, and Micah could see us through the arched doorway of the dining room. David hip-bumped me. "Shhh."

I elbowed his ribs. "*You* shush."

"I'll deal with you later," he said so only I could hear.

"Pshhh." I rolled my eyes.

I sat beside Micah and David stood behind my chair.

"How did the meeting go last night?" he asked.

Alder put his elbows on the table. "No one from your clutch really knows any witches, but Marita felt a block there like the one that had a hold of Harris."

Marita spoke up. "I was feeling stifled back home, and that has only intensified here. When we met with the clutch, I couldn't read anyone. I couldn't see their auras. Vampires prove more difficult, but there's always *something* there."

"I think there is a powerful hedge witch here," Trace declared.

A light went off in my head. Hedge witches communicated with the spiritual world. They also practiced astral projection. I thought about the night I was dreaming about being in David's office, then suddenly, I was physically there. He and I both knew it happened. David's hand sweetly rubbed my shoulder. We were thinking the same thing. We hadn't told anyone else about it. But then my mind went further into realization, or speculation, I wasn't sure which. I jumped up from my chair.

"Trace, can we talk? David, may we use your office?"

"Of course."

I shut the door and Trace sat on the sofa. I paced the floor. What I was thinking was wild. I mean, way out there.

"Willa! Out with it!"

"Okay, okay. So, a hedge witch. A hedge witch may be fucking with us and that in and of itself is bad because they can sometimes use the spirit world against us, but also there's the whole astral projection thing. Say they wanted to hurt us, so they project somewhere near, throw down a curse, and leave. *Or!* Or they could even use the spirits to watch us, and they would know everything we do and everyone we are with. No one would ever be safe."

I sounded manic spilling out my thoughts and then I plopped down beside Trace on the couch and slapped my hands on my knees. "Trace, I think I'm a hedge witch."

She shook her head. "Wait. What? You mean the dreams? Because I don't know what they are, but I'm not sure..."

"Trace, I was here. In this office. With David. It started as a dream. It was only for about ten minutes, and it only happened once, but I was here. He knows it too."

She studied my face. "That means...I mean, probably...your..."

"My mother or father was a witch. Or is..."

Trace stared straight ahead. "Damn."

"And now I'm thinking, what if it's one of my parents? Doing...whatever it is they're trying to do. I never met my dad and Mom took off so long ago, I just, I don't know."

I could tell her thoughts were coming faster than she could

process. Then, I had a truly terrible pondering. I began to cry because my gut told me the realization could be very true.

"Willa, what is it?"

I wiped my wet cheeks. "If my mother or father has hurt anyone we love, I don't know what I'll do."

There was a knock at the door, then it opened. Harris, Alder, Micah, and David entered. Alder sat beside me and grabbed my hand. "Willa, I heard your thoughts. They were loud in my head."

"That's probably because I'm freaking out a little bit here." I stood up. "I can go somewhere. Leave. Maybe if I'm not in the picture, they will leave you all alone."

Micah shook his head. "No way. Nope. You're not going anywhere."

"Willa, you don't know *who* is involved. Nothing is certain. I won't let you go either," David firmly stated.

I gasped. "*Let* me?" I planted myself in front of David, tilting my chin up. We were nose to nose. "Don't you understand? I would rather be far away, all alone, than see anyone harmed." My voice softened. "That includes you, David."

Passion filled his glowing eyes. "And that's exactly the sentiment we hold for you, sweet Willa. You're stuck with us. All of us."

"We're in this together," Harris declared.

Trace hugged me. "Yeah, what if they came after us anyway and we needed you, but you weren't here?"

"You've already played a huge part in saving me," Harris added.

I squeezed Trace. "Okay, okay. We'll figure this out."

I felt Alder's hand on my back. I turned to him, and he kissed me sweetly.

"What do you need right now?" he whispered in my ear.

I looked up at my mate. Love bubbled within my heart.

"The big picture? I need everyone in this house. Right now? I'd like to spend a little time grounding myself with Micah."

Alder kissed my nose and nodded.

MICAH

Being needed by Willa meant everything to me. She was quiet as I shut the door to our room. Her hands glowed as soon as our eyes met. I held up my hands and she placed her palms to mine, lacing our fingers together.

"Close your eyes."

Willa smiled and shook her head no.

"*Close your eyes.*"

She gave me a peck on the lips before I could protest, not that I would, sighed, and then complied. I wanted to kiss her back. Let my tongue explore her pouty mouth. Run my hands all over her body, but I used all my willpower not to.

"Concentrate on each breath. Stop thinking about what you want to do to me." We couldn't help but laugh a little. "Okay, seriously. Do you feel the rug under your feet?"

"Yes," she whispered.

"Feel my energy flowing into your palms? Pull it in. Absorb the light I give you. It comes from my most loving and devoted soul, Willa. I'm wholeheartedly in love with you. I'm completely devoted to you. Pull me into you and let me fill you. Push darkness down into the floor."

Willa's vibrations were palpable for a minute, then they subsided. She panted a few times, releasing negativity, and opened her eyes. She grabbed me around the waist and buried her face in my chest. I held on so tight. I held on as long as she needed. I had an eternity to live, and I would spend it holding my Willa if that's what she wanted. Then I read her mind and my fangs descended.

"You don't have to," I said.

Willa swooped her hair over one shoulder, exposing her beautiful, tantalizing neck. "I want to. I need to." Her head tilted and I listened to her pulse. "Taste me again, Micah."

I held her shoulders and slowly walked her back to the bed where I gently laid her down. I roamed her shape through thin leggings from ankles to hips. I dug my fingers in then continued

83

up to cup her breasts. I squeezed. She whimpered, found the hem of my t-shirt, and yanked it up. I peeled it off and threw it wherever. She sat up and I ripped her blouse open. Buttons went flying.

Her eyes burned. "I have to have your skin against mine. Friction, goosebumps, nerve endings, energy, and hearts beating together. Devoted," she almost chanted.

I pushed her back down and put my fingertips on the place I would have my drink. "Oh, I'm devoted."

Willa closed her eyes, and I sank in. Fangs, body, and soul. All of me into every molecule of her. Nothing and no one would ever taste like my Willa.

I heard the door to the room open and close, but I kept drinking. Willa's throat vibrated against my mouth. "Hello, my love," she affectionately said to Alder. Her heart rate remained steady. I sucked once more then licked the wound. Willa sighed.

Alder stood naked by the bed. "Dawn will break soon. We should rest." I rolled over and Willa pressed herself to my chest. Alder held on to her from behind and we were complete.

Sixteen

WILLA

I slept as long as I could. The sun hadn't quite gone down when I rolled myself over Micah and got out of bed. He scooted in to spoon Alder. I leaned down and whispered to them, "It's not yet time. Rest a little longer."

I got dressed, brushed my teeth, and walked the silent hall. Making coffee alone was nice, but I wasn't alone in my thoughts. The last time everyone saw me, I had made such a spectacle. And David's birthday had come and gone. How selfish I was. The mug warmed my hands as I sipped and slowly meandered again. The door to David's office was now closed. It had been open before. I held my ear to the door but heard nothing at first.

"Come in, Willa," David called, and I jumped, almost spilling my coffee.

Of course, he read my mind and knew I was there. I went inside. He sat at his desk looking very professorish in slacks and a white button down. I put my mug on a coaster on the coffee table in front of the sofa and went to him. I boldly climbed onto his lap. He looked surprised. I felt like he needed some taking care of.

Some alone time. I curled up on his chest and he wrapped his arms around me.

"What are all of these thoughts about, babe?"

"Don't you already know?"

"You didn't ruin my birthday. I don't even know why I told you. I never expect anyone to fuss over it. I should have kept it to myself."

I sat up and looked into his eyes. "I'm happy you told me. It makes me feel special when you share things with me."

David's hand slid from my waist to my bottom. "Willa, you don't need me to make you special. You are an anomaly. A magical bewitching being and don't let your intrusive thoughts convince you otherwise."

My lips ached to touch his. His lips that spoke such beautiful words about me. Words he sincerely meant. He pulled me in and kissed me. Appeasing me. Setting the rest of me on fire. We kissed for a long while and when his fangs descended, he stopped. We were both extremely turned on, but now wasn't the time. I panted. "Thank you for that."

He laughed. "I've wanted to kiss you like that ever since you left me bent over my bed. Don't get me wrong, I loved every second of it."

"I would offer you a little drink, but Micah had his fill last night and I really need to eat first."

David lifted me off of his lap. "Well then, let's see if Marco is up. His omelets are to die for."

"I'm still getting used to eating breakfast after dark," I joked. The scent of bacon made my stomach growl. David heard it and squeezed my hand that was in his. I heard the others talking and laughing. My eyes met Micah's as we rounded the corner, then everything went black.

MICAH

"There you two are," I said just as Willa vanished into thin air. I froze. "Willa? Where'd she go?"

"*What the fuck?*" Harris exclaimed.

A pan clattered to the tile floor when Marco dropped it.

David examined his hands as if he had never seen them before then looked all around. "She was...she was just here holding my hand. Where the fuck is she? Willa! Babe?"

We were all at a loss. Alder turned to Marita. "I can't hear her. Do you feel her presence?"

Marita closed her eyes. "Just hold on. Give me a second."

Trace looked bewildered and I hugged her. Our best friend was gone in an instant. She held on to me tight. "I don't feel her energy, but I think I'm too shocked to tell."

Marita opened her eyes and shook her head. "I'm getting nothing."

Alder and David ran outside to look around, even though I knew they would find nothing. They returned looking defeated.

WILLA

My head pounded. Where did everyone go? I no longer smelled bacon. It was quiet. Where the fuck was I? I bolted upright and looked around. I immediately got dizzy. A single lamp gave light in a small space that looked a lot like Alder's flat. I was on a sofa. Movement to the left caught my attention. There was a tall figure with its back to me. Sharp pain stabbed my temple. I groaned and the figure turned around.

"Lie back down. I promise it will help."

The man came near and offered a glass of water. His accent was American. I noticed his eyes first. They were green, like mine. His hair was auburn, like mine. Even the shape of his nose was just like mine. I reluctantly took the glass and sipped then reclined back against the cushions.

"I'd rather have coffee. And who the fuck are you?"

He laughed at me wickedly and forced my legs to move over as he sat beside me. He held out a hand and it glowed for a brief moment. My eyes went wide.

"Who...the fuck...are you?"

"My name is Wesley. I'm your twin."

I dropped the glass, and it shattered on the floor.

"Where have you been? How...how did you find me?"

"Oh, I've always known about you. And let me tell you, the things you do with those blood suckers is fucking disgusting."

I gasped. "You spying on me like that sounds pretty fucking disgusting! What the hell is wrong with you? I'm guessing you hate vampires," I scoffed. "How did you get me here?"

"I'm powerful, Willa. I have embraced what I am. You should too. I can teach you. We could rule the darkness."

I shook my head. "We? No thanks."

I pushed past the headache and sat up, attempting to push him up and out of the way. He grabbed my shoulders and easily held me in place. The look on his face scared me.

"Not so fast, sweetheart. You and I belong together." His hand caressed my cheek, and his eyes were wild with lust. Before I could think, he had a firm hold on my chin and crushed his lips to mine. His tongue shoved between my lips, and I bit down on it. He let out a terrible sound, pulled back, and slapped me hard across my face, then jumped up and paced in circles, flexing his fingers. I swear he almost broke my jaw. I cried. I couldn't stop myself. The pain was too much. I didn't dare move out of fright. Wesley spit blood onto the wood floor and wiped his mouth.

"You bitch. I'll kill you if you try that again."

I knew he would and not think twice. I flinched and my words came out jumbled. "I won't. I won't. I promise." I didn't look at him. It hurt to speak.

He sat back down looking utterly angry with me. "Good. Don't. You'll realize, in time, what we can be."

I barely moved my lips. "In time? I can't stay here. You can't keep me here. I belong with Alder."

Wesley stood and paced again. "That's bullshit, Willa. Vampires seduced you. They glamoured you."

"I swear, it's not like that. And anyway, where have you been? How did I not know about you?"

"You were with mother, well, until she left. I'm not surprised she left. She was a selfish whore who didn't want us in the first place. One of her jealous lovers killed her, you know. You were much better off with Trace's grandmother."

"So, were you with our father?"

"Yes. He encouraged me to embrace what I am when I was old enough. To become a strong witch."

"A hedge witch?"

Wesley sat back down. "That's how I've been watching you. Spirits are surprisingly useful. And they don't bitch and complain. They're just happy to be occupied. I haven't mastered astral projection myself just yet, so I use the spirits."

The fact that he didn't know how to astral project was good news for me, but how had he gotten me here? Was it magic, a spell? Maybe, if I could control my abilities, I was more powerful than he thought. Did he know I had done it before? He couldn't have been watching me every second of the day, could he? If not, it might save me. *If* I could control it, that is. My stomach turned thinking about him creeping on me with my mates. What a sick and twisted individual. And kissing his twin sister! I would die if he tried to go any further with me than he already had. His anger only fueled his strength. I may not be able to fend him off on my own.

Seventeen

MICAH

David sat at the desk while the rest of us paced around his office. Marita searched her laptop for information on witch covens in London since the Kingswood clutch didn't associate with any.

"We have to find the most experienced witch around," she stated. "One who extensively knows about other hedge witches."

"Astral projection is different than abducting someone out of thin air, right?" Trace asked.

"Yes. That's why I'm almost certain Willa didn't do this herself. But a hedge witch may have knowledge about the kind of powerful spell required to physically take someone without their consent."

Just then, the doorbell rang, and we all looked at each other suspiciously. This was a house of vampires, and it was the middle of the night. Marco looked at David who stood. "Let's both go," David said.

They went, but the rest of us followed. David looked at us over his shoulder.

"Hey, we're all in this together," I said. "I'm surprised you don't have a command center with high tech surveillance or something."

"Well, I've never needed it."

David pulled out his phone and clicked on an app. There were no windows near the front door, so whoever was standing on the other side had no idea we were all there.

"Hmm," David pondered. "Never seen this bloke before."

He showed us the phone screen. One man stood there alone. He looked impatient, then banged his fist hard on the door. David spoke through his cell.

"Who the bloody hell are you? It's a little late to be banging on my door."

"Jude. Jude Deberry."

Trace gasped.

"Can I?" Alder asked David who handed him the phone.

"You're Willa's father. Do you know where she is?"

Jude shook his head. "No, but I have an idea who has her. Please let me in and I will explain."

I looked at Alder apprehensively. He patted my shoulder.

"It's fine. He's the human walking into a house full of vampires."

David opened the door and Jude came in. David led us to the big dining room table. I didn't sit. I was full of energy. Jude wasted no time, and I was glad.

"I believe Willa is with her brother. She has a twin brother."

None of us knew how to respond.

"I take it none of you have ever heard of Wesley. I'm a witch. As was the twins' mother, Shia. She was a wild soul. I wasn't enough. The children weren't enough. I tried to take Willa with me, but she refused. Not for Willa's sake, but to hurt me."

"Willa said her mother left when she was very young," I said.

"Yes. Her promiscuity and the energy she gave off got her killed. An obsessed lover who became addicted with her murdered her. I found Willa and she seemed happy enough, so I didn't disrupt her life further. But...Wesley. I taught him how to be a witch. A good one. A powerful one, but he had a rebellious streak. Our coven grew tired of him wanting to bend the rules and push their boundaries. They wanted to discipline him, so he left eleven years ago. A coven is important. The accountability is necessary for people with any kind of power to stay humble and to stay safe. A lone witch is dangerous. And Wesley has something in his possession that dramatically increases that danger."

"What?" Marita asked.

"A stone. He found it after a meteor shower when he was a kid. I never paid it much mind, but when he turned sixteen, he started wearing it around his neck. That's when he began acting out. The coven wanted it destroyed. I examined it once when he was asleep and I swear, it was like peering into a black hole. He calls it the void."

"That sounds fucking creepy, and what the hell does he want with Willa?" I demanded.

"Yes, I'd also like to know," Alder stated. I could tell he was angry or just running out of patience.

"He knows she has taken up with vampires. Wesley hates your kind. Please know, I don't have anything against you."

"Why does he care?" I asked. "It's not like he's been around, and Willa would have loved having a brother."

"I'm not sure, to be honest. Sometimes I think he's got nothing better to do."

Harris spoke up. "Surely he doesn't think he has a chance against all of us?"

Alder propped his elbows on the table and put his face in his palms. "It won't matter if he hurts Willa before we can get to him, does it?"

"So, you can astral project too, right?" Trace asked Jude.

"I can. I came here for protection. I want to see if I can find her through projection, but I need someone to be near my physical body when I attempt it."

"I'll do it," Marita spoke up. "I'm very good at reading energy.

I shouldn't have a problem recognizing if you are in distress, but how can I help if you are?"

"You lay hands on me. Concentrate and send your energy to me."

Marita nodded. "Trace can help too."

"Of course I can. I'll do anything to get Willa back."

"And thank you for being there for her all of these years. You two were destined to be friends from the beginning," Jude said. "I think I'll try to project for a short time to see if I can tell where they are and assess the situation, unless Willa's in immediate danger, of course."

"Yes, that's probably for the best," added David. "Dawn is coming soon."

Marita stood. "We can do this while you rest. A protection spell beforehand should help. I promise we will be safe."

WILLA

I rubbed my jaw and watched Wesley gather up a towel, latex gloves, and a small box.

"Alright. Time for a change," he said as he wrapped the towel around my shoulders. The box was permanent hair color in blonde.

"Why are you doing this?" I asked quietly while he put on the gloves. I didn't want to upset him. He began dying my hair.

"It's crazy, right? I can poof you here right out of thin air, but I can't change your hair color with the snap of my fingers. Why am I doing this? Why? Because you'll look less like me, for one. And...maybe, just maybe, your bloodsuckers won't notice you at first glance if they are near."

But they would know it's me. They can feel me. They can read my mind, but I kept these glimmers of hope to myself and let him continue. When he finished, he poured us both some wine.

"We've got about forty-five minutes until we rinse. Might as well relax. Rest that jaw of yours. I am sorry I had to do that, but you made me. You have to be a good girl for me, Willa." Wesley slid his hand from my knee up my thigh. Thankfully, he stopped before going further. "There will be plenty of time to get to know each other more intimately later."

The thought made me want to throw up and suddenly the wine tasted sour on my tongue, but I kept sipping.

"After we get done with your hair, you need to sleep. Get you back on human time."

I didn't protest because I was tired as hell and the wine only added to that. I was also hoping I could dream. I wanted to see what was happening at David's house. If I could project, I could speak with David and at least tell him who had me. Energy swirled within me, and I kept it tamped down so I could use every bit when I needed it the most, but my body felt weak, and I realized I hadn't eaten in a long time.

"I'm hungry. Can I have something to eat?" I asked meekly.

Wesley jumped up. "Yes, of course. I'll heat you up some soup. Shouldn't hurt too much."

After eating, he sent me into the bathroom and told me to take a shower to wash out the hair dye. I gasped when I saw my face. A dark bruise shadowed the lower left side, and it was swollen. My mates would tear Wesley limb from limb if they saw me like this. I let myself cry it out in the shower, then blow dried my new golden locks and redressed in the same clothes I had on before. When I came out, Wesley had thrown a pillow and blanket onto the couch. He wasn't even decent enough to offer me the bed, but I guessed it was because the bed was closer to the door out of the flat. At least he wasn't making me sleep with him.

"That color suits you. Get some rest and don't try anything funny. There's an alarm on the door."

I didn't say anything. I lay down, concentrated all of my energy on thoughts of David's home, and went to sleep.

Eighteen

WILLA

Floating above a scene never felt normal. I suppose I shouldn't expect it to, and it probably never would, but I wasn't in David's room. Alder and Micah were spooning below me. I willed my body to move. My hands glowed and I imagined they were magnets seeking out my mates. Closer. It was working. Just a little bit farther. I extended my fingers out, desperately hoping to touch Micah who was inches away. I closed my eyes with a final stretch and felt his curls. I opened my eyes and he mumbled but wasn't awake yet. I managed to kneel beside the bed and held on to the comforter, afraid my body might float away. I leaned down to whisper into his ear.

"Micah, it's me."

He flipped over so fast. "Willa?"

I grabbed his face and kissed him. He wrapped me up in his arms. "Willa, how did you get here?"

"Don't let go of me. I'm projecting, so I don't think I'll be here long. I shouldn't stay away for long anyway." Alder was still asleep. "Micah, I have a twin. His name is Wesley, and he is a witch too. He's got me in a flat that looks like Alder's. That's all I know."

He looked me over in the dim light. "Are you blonde? What's going on?"

I kept the left side of my face in the shadows. I didn't want him to see my bruise. "He dyed it. He wants me to stay with him. Please, be careful. He hates true vampires and he's powerful, Micah. I don't know what he's capable of. I need to get back."

He didn't let go. "Wait. Willa, there's so much to tell you."

"I can't right now. I have to go. Let go, Micah. I promise, I'll come back, if I can. Look for Wesley. I love you. Tell Alder I love him." And I disappeared like a mist out of his embrace.

MICAH

"No! Willa, wait," I yelled.

Alder jumped up from the bed. "Willa? What the bloody hell is going on? Is Willa here?"

I slumped over. "No. I mean, not any more. She was right here though for a few minutes. She projected to me." I jumped up. "We have to tell the others. Isn't Jude trying to project to her?"

Alder grabbed my arm. "Hold on. It's still day time for another hour or so."

He cracked the door open to make sure the windows and doors were securely covered from the light. "Okay. We're good. Let's get David."

Alder knocked a few times, but we heard nothing. I impatiently stepped in front of him and banged on the door.

"Alright. I'm coming!" David opened the door naked and sleepy eyed. "What time is it?"

"Willa came to me," I blurted out. That brought him out of his haze.

"Just now?"

"Yes, but she's gone. We're going to see if Jude has succeeded in reaching her," Alder replied.

As David pulled on his sweatpants, we heard the witches chanting. We followed their voices to the living room.

Life to life
And mind to mind
Your spirits now
Will intertwine
You join your souls
And journey together
To let your eyes see
Share truths unknown

Jude lay still in the middle of the rug on the floor as Marita and Trace continued their words on loop. Alder, David, and I stood watching and waiting. Harris and Marco quietly joined us in the doorway. None of us crossed the threshold for fear of disturbing them.

Harris mouthed the words to me, "We heard you banging on a door." I shrugged and motioned toward the witches.

Marita touched Jude's temples and Trace placed her palms on the bottoms of his feet. My toes tingled as his body began to vibrate, sending waves of energy across the floor. Marita nodded at Trace as if to confirm it was working. After only a few minutes, Jude's eyes popped open. We all gasped. Trace looked at me and nodded. I rushed over and helped Jude sit up. Vibrations still pulsed from his hand to mine. He opened his mouth a couple of times, but no words came out.

"Take your time," I told him.

"Water," he whispered. Marco ran to grab some.

Marita took the hand I wasn't holding as Jude drank from the cup she offered.

"Slowly. It takes a lot out of you to do what you did. Gather the energy you feel circling and try to slow it down. Deep breaths. Relax. You can tell us everything when you are ready and then we are getting you tucked into bed for a long rest," Marita soothed. It reminded me of all of the times I soothed Willa and helped her get grounded.

His eyes readjusted to his surroundings. Marita and I helped him up to sit on the couch.

"Did you see Willa?" I asked.

"I saw her. Laying on a sofa. Wesley was in the bed," he barely got out as he began to cry.

Alder kneeled in front of him. "What is it? Was she okay? She's alive?"

"Yes, yes," he sobbed. "But he's hurt her. Wesley has a temper. He's hit her. I saw her face."

Alder growled and anger welled up within me. Anger like I'd never felt before. More rage than I had experienced with Cateline. How had I not noticed her wounds when she had come to me?

"Do you have any idea where they are?" Alder pleaded.

"Yes, I...I backed out. Above. I took myself through the top. The top of the building. I think I can find it. I saw the building."

Alder's head dropped in relief. "Oh, thank you." He looked into Jude's eyes. "Thank you." Then he looked at Marita and Trace. "Thank you too."

I went to Trace and hugged her tight. "We'll get her," I promised. I promised to Trace and to the others and most of all to myself.

Nineteen

WILLA

Sadness hit me out of nowhere when I woke up. Sadness that I was here, away from everyone I loved. Sadness when I thought about all of the years I wished for family. Blood family. And to find out I had a twin who was very obviously twisted and evil pained me to the core. I touched my lips where I could still feel the sensation of Micah's mouth. The smell of his breath remained in my mind. I wished his arms were around me in that moment. I wished I was between him and Alder, cuddled up, safe in the bed.

Wesley stirred and brought me out of my thoughts. It was dark outside. I needed to have my wits about me but wanted to appear weak so that maybe he wouldn't be so harsh. I had to buy time. I had to figure out where we were. I pretended to still be asleep, and Wesley went straight into the bathroom and turned on the shower.

I got up, went to the front door, and stood there. I stared at it. My fingers wrapped around the cool brass knob, and I was so tempted to turn it, but I resisted the urge. Wesley was more than capable of beating me black and blue. I looked around the small flat, and thanked the universe there was a coffee maker, so I searched the cabinets and drawers and found everything I needed. I made a full pot and poured two mugs full.

Wesley came out with wet hair, shirtless, and wearing black jeans. I offered a small fake smile and the mug of coffee.

"I wasn't sure how you take it."

He had a wide grin. "Black. Thanks."

Of course his evil ass took it black, I thought. When he sat next to me at the small kitchen table, I noticed the stone he wore on a black chain. It was as dark as night with glints of silver or...I wasn't sure. It looked like twinkling lights. Like stars in the night sky on an infinite background. Mesmerizing. He noticed me looking closer. He leaned near.

"You like the void? So do I. I never take it off."

"The void?"

Wesley caressed it and licked his lips. "Mmm." He closed his hand around it. "The void holds power you can't imagine, Willa."

I imagined it to be pretty fucking sinister the way he treated it.

"Where did you get it?"

He sighed wistfully. "Oh, it was given to me by the universe itself. And I was only an innocent eleven-year-old boy. I had no idea how special I was. Father hadn't told me about witches, even though we lived with a coven. I just thought they were all bohemian relatives, but one day I got angry with another child while we were playing. He took my bike and taunted me with it. He said he wouldn't give it back. That it was his. My chest vibrated. My hands shook and when I grabbed his arm, he screamed and fell straight to the ground. It was like I had struck him with lightning. And don't get me wrong, I was scared too. I ran to Father."

Every time Wesley said father I cringed. Why did most villains use the word father? He continued.

"I guess he had to explain after that. Finally knowing why I had always felt different changed everything for me. I begged Father to teach me, and he did, but don't blame him for any of this. He only taught me to be good and decent. The void helped me to see what else I could be."

I hesitated to speak, but he paused. He wanted me to ask.

"And...what is that?"

His eyes were black when he answered.

"I am the void. Pride, greed, wrath, envy, lust, gluttony, and sloth. All rolled into one perfect evil entity."

What he said chilled me to the bone. "Do you think the stone gave you power?"

He stood and lifted my chin to look into the blackness of his gaze. Muddied negative energy crept down my neck from his touch. "I told you, Willa. I'm the void. I'm the god of everything humanity is afraid of."

"Then why do you need me?"

"Don't you see? We are made the same. Birthed into magic. If we were made one flesh in every sense of the word and I taught you what you truly are, we could subjugate the world."

I was at a loss. I didn't know what to say or what to do. Was he completely crazy? Was he as powerful as he claimed? It could go either way, but I kept thinking about all of the people I loved. I had to keep them safe.

Wesley took my mug and put it in the sink.

"That's enough for now. You should try and get some more sleep. Get you back on human time, remember?"

He took rope from a drawer and walked toward me.

"Wait. What's that for? I won't try anything funny."

He slid his hands down my arms and gently pulled them behind my back, then proceeded to bind them from my elbows down to my wrists.

"I have to go out for a bit, and I can't have you misbehaving." He twisted my body onto my side and lay me down, then covered me with the blanket. "You're not going to get loud, are you? I'll stuff your mouth, if so."

I freaked out. I'd choke to death if he did that.

"No. I promise. I swear I'll be good."

"Do try to get some rest, Willa," he said as he left.

I closed my eyes.

DAVID JUMPED up from sitting behind his desk when he saw me floating by the door. My arms weren't bound here, and he pulled me down to him when I reached for his hand. He held on to me and I latched onto him.

"Oh, love. I'm so happy you came to me. We have to find you, babe. Do you have any more information that will help?"

He put a little space between us and looked at my bruise. I touched it, self-consciously. David placed his lips there with a feathery light touch. "What has he done to you? I'm going to kill him."

"I'm okay. I promise. I can't stay long. I really do think I'm in the same building with Alder's flat. Search there, but please be careful. Wesley is crazy. He's evil. I think it's that stone he wears. We have to get rid of it somehow, but he never takes the damn thing off."

"Do you think you can wait until tomorrow night? Dawn will come soon."

"Yes. I can. I think I can."

David kissed me and hugged me again. We both startled when Alder and Harris burst through the door.

"Micah's gone," Alder exclaimed. Then he saw me. "Willa?"

I jolted awake again. My shoulders throbbed from the position I was in. Alder had said Micah was gone. I panicked. What had Wesley done?

Twenty

WILLA

The door to the flat opened and I heard Wesley grunting. I heaved myself up to sit so I could see what was going on. I bit my lip to keep from shrieking as I watched Wesley drag Micah's limp body across the floor. What the fuck? The sun was rising. Micah couldn't be here. Wesley kept dragging him until he was on the other side of the bed, in the shadows, dropping his heels to the floor with a loud thump, and left him there.

"That will do for now." He looked at me. "Aww, what's wrong, Willa. You should see your face. Surprise!"

I tasted bile, my stomach turned, and I threw up.

"Oh no. You're weak Willa."

I cried. "Why? Why are you doing this?"

Wesley kicked Micah's foot, but he didn't move.

"The bloodsuckers have to go. They've corrupted you. They think they're better than witches, you know. Vampires only want to mate with witches for our blood. It's like a drug to them. They don't really give a shit about you. Your blood and your energy feed them. And that's going to stop."

I was afraid to ask, but I did anyway. "Is he dead?"

"No. Not yet." Wesley untied my wrists and sat beside me. "Don't try anything." He pointed at the vomit on the floor. "You'll be cleaning that up." He scooted close and put an arm around me. "You and I will be one." He traced a finger over my collar bone. "It can only be you." His eyes were black again. "I'll get rid of them one by one until you accept your fate and surrender completely to me."

I desperately wanted to run to Micah and throw myself on top of him. "Please don't do this. Please," I begged.

Wesley dismissed my words. "Go get yourself cleaned up. There's a new toothbrush on the sink."

I looked at Micah's lifeless body when I walked to the bathroom and my hope faded. I wept when I was alone. I covered my mouth with my hand so that Wesley wouldn't hear me. I was in a nightmare.

TRACE

First Willa and now Micah was gone who knows where. I kept thinking one thought. Who would be next? It ran through my mind over and over. Marita suggested that Harris, Alder, David, and Marco rest in the same room along with one of us. That way we could watch out for one another as best we could. We cast protection lines across every door and window of David's home with red and black salt. Marita volunteered to stay with the vampires while Jude and I drove around London to look for the building Jude had observed while projecting. Willa told David to search near Alder's flat, so we headed there first.

JUDE DROVE HIS BMW. There was silence for a little while, then he finally spoke.

"Thank you for always being there for my Willa. I regret not being in her life. I hate that I left her with her mother, but she never would have met you if I had taken her with me."

"I don't know what I would do without her. We have to find her, and she has to be okay. Micah too. Willa needs him."

Jude parked, and we stood in front of the red brick building for a few moments. People walked in and out of the lobby like it was any other cloudy boring day. I tucked a stray strand of red hair under the edge of my beanie to make sure it didn't show. Jude wore a baseball cap. We didn't want to stand out while we creeped around the place like criminals. It was nice having Jude. He was so much like me and Willa. He understood how much our own energy and the energy from others affected us. We looked at each other and I took his hand in mine to show him that we were in this together as we entered.

"I guess we find the lift," Jude suggested.

I took deep breaths once we were in the elevator. Jude squeezed my hand.

"We're only looking around. Six floors. Should we start at the top or bottom?"

"Top," I answered. He pushed the six.

I knew there would be a ding, but I still jumped at the sound.

"Alright," Jude said nervously. "Why don't you get out your cell and have a message typed in, ready to send to Marita, if needed."

"What should I say?"

"Hmm, type in our location and maybe...help needed stat, in all caps."

"Oh, that's good."

We slowly made our way down the hall, stopping at each door to listen and see if we could feel the energy. It was a little over-whelming. This building with so many people emanated emotions like a downpour of rain and my mood was getting soaked. On the third floor, I stepped out of the elevator and leaned against the wall. Jude propped up next to me.

"Halfway through," he sighed.

"I feel like a sponge. A soggy one. I hope a quick getaway won't be necessary because it will be like running through mud."

He laughed a little. "I'll drag you out if I have to."

"Alright. Shall we continue?"

Nothing so far, but the fluorescent lighting on the second floor appeared dimmer than the rest of the place. Energy often affected lights and electricity.

"I think we may be near," Jude whispered.

We heard shouting behind the second door we came to, and I put my ear to it. A couple argued loudly. "That's not Willa."

We moved from door to door. The next to the last one, 222, stopped us in our tracks. It had an extra lock and a very expensive security system equipped with a camera. I turned around quickly, pulling Jude behind me. Maybe I could high tail it out of there faster than I thought.

"Hurry up hurry up," I said to the elevator like it could hear me.

We briskly made our way back through the lobby and out to Jude's car. He immediately locked the doors and we both let out our breath.

"I think we found it," Jude said with conviction.

"Oh my god. I could never be a private investigator or a spy. I just hope Micah is in there too."

I looked at the building again before we pulled away, thinking about my best friend being held inside.

Twenty-One

MICAH

I had faced death before and it felt just like this. I couldn't believe it was happening again. But would I make it this time? Would this be the end? My end?

I blinked. My limbs were heavy. I couldn't even move my fingers. I knew I was no longer lying next to Alder. The room was filled with natural light, and I freaked out. Even in cloudy London, I'd never make it in the sunlight. I tried to get my fangs to descend, but they wouldn't.

"Oh look. You're awake," Wesley sneered, peering into my gaze. I knew it was him. He had Willa's eyes, and the rest of his features were pretty damn close too.

He was the last person I wanted to see. He wore a shit eating grin and I wanted to tell him to fuck off, but all I could do was blink again. He cackled then his eyes went as black as a starless sky. He grabbed my cheeks and pinched them together hard like he was about to force feed me his next words.

"I watched what you did with my sister. She's mine now." He stopped squeezing my cheeks and lifted my upper lip. "Aww, no fangs? Not so scary now, are you?" He played with my hair. "You are beautiful."

I heard an audible gasp. "Micah?"

Willa. My sweet Willa. I felt her draped over my chest. Her hands ran across my body like she was making sure I was really there. I wished I could hold onto her. Then the weight of her was gone in an instant and I heard her tumble onto the floor.

"Enough," Wesley barked. "Don't touch him again. Get up off the floor. You're not trash. Go sit on the couch. I'll have you sitting on a throne soon."

WILLA

A throne? I wanted to laugh. I wanted to scream. I wanted to cry, but the only thing I could do at the moment was obey Wesley. I had to tread lightly, especially now that Micah was here. There would be no way to stop Wesley from ending Micah in the state he was in. And I needed to get that fucking stone off of Wesley's neck.

TRACE

Marita let us in when we returned. The vampires were all accounted for and still asleep in David's theater room.

"We think we found it, but I have no idea if Micah is there. I just couldn't judge the energy," I told her.

"And there's a pretty good security system, so we had to leave before anyone noticed us prying," Jude added.

"That's amazing you found it," she beamed. "We will make a solid plan with the others at dusk. I've been researching powerful protection spells, and Jude, I'm sure you have a lot of experience to offer."

"Of course. I'll do anything and everything in my power. I wish Willa knew what magic she has. I would project to her again and tell her to realize it, but I think it's too dangerous to try and contact her. Wesley would surely see me."

"Yeah, I'm afraid this is going to have to be a sneak attack. Totally surprise him," I said.

Marita nodded. "If you two will stay here, I want to go to Wicca Moon before they close to get some things we may need."

"Will you grab enough rosemary sprigs and string for each of us to wear around our necks?" Jude looked at me. "Vampires don't mind rosemary, do they?"

I laughed. "No, I think it's fine."

He shrugged. "I know it sounds like a small thing, but the basics can be quite effective against negativity."

Marita left and Jude and I quietly entered the theater room. I sat on the floor, next to where Harris lay on a pallet. He grumbled and turned over to put his arm around my waist. His nose nuzzled my hip.

"Everything okay?" he mumbled.

"Yes. Rest," I whispered.

Jude sprawled on the empty sofa on the back row of the stadium style seating. "I'm going to try to nap. We may have a long night ahead of us."

MARCO WAS the first vampire to wake. He stretched like a cat and shuffled to the door. "I'm going to change clothes and whip up something to eat for you humans."

Harris tugged me down beside him and kissed my nose.

"Good evening, love. We have a big night ahead. Do you think Jude is prepared to see Wesley killed, because it's highly likely," Harris warned.

I sighed. "What a dreadful thought. But I know you're right. One child is in danger from the other child. It must be hard."

Harris hugged me. "Maybe Alder can talk to him before all of this goes down."

Marco stuck his head back in. "Come eat, you crazy kids."

Marita hummed from the living room where she worked, setting up a small altar and getting protection spells ready. The rest of us were in the kitchen. We were all quietly eating. The vampires sipped on blood. Marco refilled their cups.

"A little extra tonight," he said.

David stood at the head of the table and ran a hand through his dark hair. "I'm not sure what the right thing to say here is...but I wanted to offer a few words."

Marita came and leaned on the door frame to listen.

"My life as the London primus has been easy. Threats like this have never surfaced in my time, but the Kingswood clutch will be on alert and around the area of the building. I've never had to imagine losing someone I loved." He looked at Alder. "I love Willa and I promise to get her back to you. Whatever it takes."

We all knew he meant that he would sacrifice himself if he had to. Then he turned to Jude. "Just because you weren't around, doesn't mean you love your daughter any less, but if...if Wesley gets in the way..."

"I know." Jude looked around at all of our faces. "Evil must not prevail. I know that. And without giving all of the details to them, my coven is aware that Wesley is causing trouble. They are together right now and will be sending out protective energy throughout the night."

Alder gave him a nod of understanding then added, "And with everything in me, I hope Micah is there with her."

Marita clasped her hands together. "Shall we?"

I lit pure white candles. I called the corners. A circle was cast. I concentrated on all of the positive energy circling within me as I recited the words.

A spell of safety here I cast
Words of might to hold us fast
Shields before us and behind

To right and left, protection bind
To us may no harm or ill will come
By power of three our magic is from
With the sacred light around us
As above – So below, Blessed Be
"Close your eyes and circle your energy," I instructed. "Keep the good. Release the bad."

Our candle flames flickered wildly. I continued.

We call Earth to bind our spell
Air to speed its travel well
Bright as fire shall it glow
Deep as tide of water flow
Count the elements four-fold
In the fifth the spell shall hold

We closed the circle by extinguishing the flames, but Jude placed his, still burning, into a holder on the altar.

Twenty-Two

WILLA

The sun had set. Thank the universe, Micah had survived the day. David said they would come for me tonight and I didn't think Wesley had any idea. Since bringing Micah in, he seemed more full of himself than he already was. He enjoyed taunting me with Micah. It made me sick and angry. Wesley had no clue that I was storing that anger to unleash upon him when the opportunity arose.

"How long do you think a bloodsucker can go without sucking blood? Hmm? A long time, I'm guessing."

Wesley hunched over Micah to bind his ankles together. He dragged him onto the rug in front of the sofa and zip tied his wrists. Micah blinked and my heart leapt into my throat. I leaned forward to see his eyes.

"Micah!"

Wesley shoved me back. "Settle down."

Micah's eyelids fluttered. I knew he heard my voice. He parted his lips, but he didn't make any noise. Wesley sat down hard on Micah's waist and propped his elbows on his knees, and I noticed the glint of the blade of a small knife in his hand.

"What if we make him bleed? I wonder how long it takes for their blood to drain," he hissed as he stabbed the three-inch blade into Micah's neck all the way to the hilt.

"No! Stop it! Why?" I screamed. "Stop!"

Wesley looked at me with black eyes. "Shut up."

Blood slowly oozed from around the wound. As it trickled down to the rug, my heart sank. Vampires heal from wounds quickly, but with the blade left in place, Micah would bleed out. This was one of the four ways vampires could be ended. Beheading, removing the heart, burning by fire or the sun, or bleeding out. Wesley lifted himself to stand but used Micah's chest as leverage which made the blood drip faster. He looked proud of himself when he straightened to stand. I wanted to kill him. I wanted to scream, but Wesley would kill me, end Micah, and be gone before the others could get here if he decided to do so.

"Please don't do this," I begged.

"Join me."

I felt defeated. Powerless. My voice was low, "Don't you see? I'll never be what you want me to be. How could I ever join you after you've done this? I'm not evil."

He got in my face and tangled his fingers in my hair, pulling my chin up to look at him. My scalp burned and tears ran down my cheeks.

"You will, because this piece of you will be gone, then the others will be next. Trace, Alder, David, Harris, until you have no one and nothing left. A deep dark hole will be there, and I'll be the one to fill it up."

Wesley let go of my hair and sat beside me. I hated feeling his body pressed against mine. Micah lay before us. The blood was pooling up now. His blond waves were soaked red under his head and his eyes were closed. Lips that used to be full and pink were now blue. His time was running out.

Where was Alder? I needed him. Like now.

Wesley had a look of madness on his face. Black eyes and that twisted smile. He leaned forward with his forearms on his thighs to watch my mate slowly slip away. What if I grabbed his throat as hard as I could and didn't let go? Maybe I could latch my fingers around the black chain and strangle him that way. My gut told me neither option would have the outcome I hoped for. The lamps in the flat flickered and Wesley laughed manically. He snapped his head around to look at me again.

"Willa, Willa, Willa." He put his hand on my knee and slid it up my thigh. "I thought you were turned on by power." He squeezed my flesh and licked his lips. "I can make you feel things you've never imagined." His other hand wrapped around the back of my head, and he pulled my face close to his. "After you see what I can do, you'll be begging me to fuck you. Do you see how weak vampires are?"

I closed my eyes as he put his lips on mine.

Twenty-Three

TRACE

It felt eerie outside of the red brick building. The lobby was deserted. We could see the second floor from where we stood and watched the lights blink inside flat 222.

"Can you feel any energy from Willa or Micah," I asked Marita.

"No. The weight of negativity is too heavy."

I turned to Alder and David. "What about her thoughts? Anything there?"

"No," Alder said. "We need to hurry."

The Kingswood clutch was gathered and dispersed at various places near the building. Some casually went in, and a couple of vampires went to each floor. A few stationed themselves on the rooftop. Our group went inside next. The lobby clerk never looked up from his laptop as we made our way to the elevators.

"Wesley probably has a spell cast on the whole building," Jude said.

When we reached the second floor, we wasted no time, but when Jude touched the doorknob, he was thrown backwards.

"Of course there's a spell on the door," Marita said.

David stepped in front. "Let me. It will hurt, but it won't kill me. I hope."

WILLA

I couldn't believe it. I heard the sweetest sound I could ever hope to hear. Someone trying to open the door. Wesley stopped kissing me and looked surprised. I took the opportunity to make my move. I used every bit of disgust that had built up inside me while his vile tongue assaulted mine and lunged forward. I straddled his chest and with one hand, my fingers wrapped around the void. I slid my other hand through the chain, all the way to my elbow, so that Wesley would basically have to dismember me to get me off. He grabbed my waist, flipped me over, tried to toss me around to release my hold as we landed on the bed, but I wouldn't let go. I couldn't. If I did, all would be lost. Micah, me, and everyone I loved.

The door burst open, and Wesley froze with me still latched on. He struggled to breathe as I twisted my arm around the chain. His fingers desperately dug into my hips, and I began to feel his energy change to panic as he started to lose control of the situation. Alder and Harris charged us, grabbing Wesley's arms. He was pinned to the mattress, and I straddled his waist again. I still didn't let go of the void, even though it seared my palm and the chain dug into my arm. He made violent hissing and screeching noises when Trace began chanting a spell.

We send back what you intentionally sent to us
May you feel the poisonous breath you poured on to us
We send your ill intentions away from us
Back to where they came
As we will, so mote it be

Wesley threw his head back and his eyes rolled wildly as I began to speak words that came from the most convicted part of my soul.

I call my energy back to me

I call my power back to me
I call my magic back to me
Anything connected to me prospers
All disconnections will not thrive on my vibration

My hands started to glow. The void no longer burned my hand. Wesley's body now convulsed, and Marita and Jude looked at me. A moment of sadness passed through my mind, knowing what would happen next. Jude had to kill Wesley. His son.

The chain weakened and I pulled one last time with all my might. I fell to the floor with the void in my hand. Marco and Trace were right by my side.

"Now. You have to do it now," Marita called out.

We looked up to see Jude rear back and plunge a dagger into Wesley's heart. Jude looked to the ceiling and twisted the blade. I winced, then began to cry. All of my emotions were spilling forth, purging from within. Marita took the void from my grasp, and I crawled over to Alder and Harris who had released Wesley and were now kneeled down beside Micah, attempting to find any signs of life. Alder pulled his bloody head onto his lap.

"Is he gone?" I asked. "Tell me!" I demanded.

Harris helped me get closer. "Not yet. He's not turned to ash. He needs blood, but it will only help if he can drink it."

I stuck out my wrist and Alder pushed me away.

"No, Willa. You can't. You've been through too much. It would kill you," he said sternly.

Trace was there in an instant, holding out her arm.

"Take mine. I'm ready. I'm strong. Take mine."

Harris took her wrist and gently bit down, then held the wound to Micah's mouth. He didn't move. Trace adjusted the angle so that the blood dripped between his lips.

"Come closer, Willa. Talk to him. Let him hear your voice," Alder instructed.

I touched Micah's face. I ran my fingers over his model perfect eyebrows and thought about the night we met Alder. I remembered dancing with Micah and how excited he was with the new possibilities of our lives together. I remembered the first time Alder kissed Micah in front of me and how I needed both of them equally. I leaned down and spoke into Micah's ear.

"Hey, bestie. It's me. Your crazy bff who got you into this mess. You have to stay with me, okay? I didn't say you could go anywhere, did I? Micah...I need you."

I heard him swallow as he took in Trace's blood. I kept talking to him through tears.

"Yes, Micah. Drink. Hey, do you remember that night when I told you to be greedy with me? Well, now would be a good time to be greedy."

I heard Alder growl when Micah's mouth smacked against Trace's wrist as he drank deeper. "Yes. Good," Alder hummed.

After a few minutes, Harris took Trace's arm away and licked her wound. "We need someone else," he said.

"More," Micah barely whispered.

I was thrilled hearing his voice.

Jude came to offer his wrist, but I stopped him.

"Wait. You've already done so much," I said.

"I'm your father. I want to. I can't make up for the time we've lost, but I can start helping out now."

Alder bit Jude's wrist and Micah continued to get his fill. Soon his color returned, and his eyes fluttered open. Jude sat back on his heels and Alder wiped the blood from Micah's mouth. He tried to speak again, but I shushed him.

"You're back, Micah. Rest."

"I love you," he said before he closed his eyes again.

"Where's David?" I asked when I realized he wasn't anywhere to be seen. Had he stayed home? Had he not come to get me? I worried that I wasn't as important to him as I had thought.

Trace saw the look in my eyes. "Don't worry," she said. "David got the door open for us to reach you. There was a really dark spell on it to block us, but he took the brunt of it. We made him stay out in the hall to recover unless we just had to have his assistance. He's here. Marco is checking on him."

They both came in and I reached for David to sit next to me. He looked spent, even for a vampire, and I touched his face.

"Thank you for coming for me."

He kissed my forehead. "Always, babe."

We all stood around the bed as Marita placed the void into the wound where Jude's dagger had entered Wesley's heart. She and Jude slathered Wesley's body in aloe. Next, they covered him in rosemary leaves and then eucalyptus oil. Finally, they wrapped him up in the comforter and bound it from one end to the other with rope. Trace handed each of us pieces of black yarn.

"Tie a knot at one end and continue tying knots until the spell is done," she told us before she began reading.

We bind you from behind
We bind you from before
That you'll hurt our people
Never ever more
We bind you from the left
We bind you from the right
We bind you by day
And we bind you by night
We bind you from below
We bind you from above
That you may never know
The laws of life and love
We bind you with your own
Good conscience within
And so let this magic
Unfold
And spin

The lamps went out and the room was dark. A rush of air blew through the flat. The lights returned and Wesley had disappeared. The vampires from the Kingswood clutch that had been near gathered in the doorway to make sure everyone was alright, and David went to tell them what had happened. The lights in the hallway brightened, so we decided we better get out of there before whatever spell Wesley had cast lifted and the people in the building wondered what the hell was going on. The Kingswood clutch escorted all of us back to David's home to make sure we arrived unharmed.

Thankfully there were still a couple of hours of darkness left. Alder and I put Micah in the shower and cleaned him up before we all settled securely in bed. Jude went home but promised to return the next evening. I didn't want my father disappearing on me again.

Twenty-Four

MICAH

I woke up with Willa's leg latched over my hip and an arm across my chest. Her warm naked body comforted me. She still slept deeply. I heard the shower turn off and Alder emerged from the bathroom a few minutes later. He stood in front of me and smiled. His wet hair was slicked back, and he wore a towel low on his hips.

"She looks like one of those alien face huggers hooked onto you from behind," he whispered.

He carefully pulled the covers up over her exposed foot, but she woke up anyway and squeezed me with her whole body. I laughed.

"Good morning, Willa."

Alder leaned down and kissed both of our heads. "Yes, good morning, darlings."

She nuzzled her nose between my curls to pepper kisses on the back of my neck, then finally loosened her connection. Alder got dressed and left us to be alone for a little while.

"Turn over," she whined. "Let me see your face."

I did as she asked and gathered her up, pulling her leg back over my hip, facing one another this time.

"Your eyes are glowing," she said quietly. "I was so afraid I wouldn't see them glow again."

"We have to stop doing this, you know. Me almost dying."

Willa giggled. "It's not funny at all, but you being able to joke about it makes me feel a little lighter. Are you sure you want to stay with me? You didn't sign up for all of this, did you?"

"You're stuck with me."

She tightened her leg around my waist, rubbing herself against my cock, and I immediately got hard. Willa gazed into my eyes with a seductive spark and my fangs descended.

"I haven't mastered mind reading yet, Willa, but I'm feeling up to it if you are."

We both knew what it was. God, I loved this woman.

Willa kissed me, then whispered into my ear, "I want you to fuck me while you suck me."

We both moaned as I slid all the way into her. I paused there, feeling our physical bond. I kissed and sucked on the sensitive skin of her neck without biting her just yet and made my way down to the softness of her breasts. I loved Alder, but this was something only Willa could offer, and I treasured her. I rolled on top and fucked her slowly. Just the way she wanted it. We were pressed chest to chest, and I was addicted to the way her body felt underneath mine while her teeth tugged my earlobe.

"Drink me, Micah."

My fangs found their drug of choice and I took a hit. No one else tasted like Willa. Talk about ecstasy. Physically, emotionally, and spiritually. She was my ultimate high. Death couldn't keep me from her and even when it tried, she would resurrect me.

WILLA

All was right in the universe. For the time being, at least. Even with facing the most evil beings who inhabited the world, I counted myself the luckiest for having those most precious on my side.

While Micah showered, I found Trace in the kitchen with everyone else milling about for dinner. I went to her and gave her the biggest hug.

"Thank you for saving Micah. You know if Harris is ever in need..."

Harris sweetly kissed the back of my head as he walked by with his cup of warm blood. "I know you would, Willa."

Trace nodded. "Of course. I never hesitated. I love Micah, too."

"And Marita, we couldn't have done it without you," I turned, "or you, Marco."

Marco waved a hand at me from the stove where he flipped over one of his famous omelets. "Willa, you don't have to thank anyone. We are family now, mate. Forever."

I peeked over his shoulder. "Mmm, is that for me?"

The doorbell rang and I heard David welcoming my father.

"Look at all of us," Marita said. "Vampires and witches. I'm thinking we should form stronger alliances here and at home from now on. Speaking of home, I should probably head back tomorrow."

"The more people on our side, the better," David agreed as he stepped into the kitchen with Jude following. David came to stand beside me where I was about to pour myself some coffee. I slammed my mug down and surprised him by jumping into his arms. He wrapped them securely around my waist.

I loved David. And I planned on telling him the next time we were alone. Who knew one person could have so much room inside? I had always believed in soulmates, and I remembered something Gran used to tell Trace and me every day, my cup runneth over. I loosened my hold and gave David a quick peck on the lips.

"Thank you for coming for me."

"Babe, you thanked me before. You don't have to thank me again. I'll never not come for you."

"David, I'll thank you because I want to, and you deserve some appreciation." I put my hands on his face when he tried to shrug me off. "I'm serious. You're more than the famous model the public thinks they know. You're kind and good and very important to me."

"Alright, alright. Remember that when you're back in New Orleans."

A shadow passed over his eyes and my heart skipped a beat. I didn't want to think about leaving him just yet. Too much of our time here had been occupied by drama.

"Uh uh. I'm not gone yet." I spoke low so that only David could hear me. "We will be here a couple of more days. Can I come see you at the club tomorrow night?"

The light in his eyes brightened. He licked his lips.

"I'd love that, babe."

A thrill ran through me, and I slapped him on the ass to remind him of the last time we spent alone before returning to my coffee mug. I warmed my hands on the cup and crawled onto Alder's lap where he sat at the dining room table. I couldn't get enough of my mates. He played with my hair, and he knew what I had asked David.

"So, we're finally going to get you to Lust." He put his mouth to my ear. "I have to admit, it turns me on. Thinking about you with David."

Want to watch, I thought. He only smiled.

After dinner, I took Jude to the library to talk. David stopped me in the hall.

"I'll be next door, in my office. If you need me, I'll be right in."

I kissed his cheek, and he winked before shutting the library door behind me.

Jude looked nervous. I hadn't decided if I wanted a real relationship with my estranged father yet, but I needed to make sure he was okay.

"Did you get some rest today?" I asked, easing into the conversation.

"Oh, a little. I'm a bit of a night owl anyway." Jude was looking down at the kilim rug. "Listen, I hate that we finally came together this way. Being brought together through chaos isn't a very good start, but I'm so thankful we're here now," he said. Then, his eyes raised to me. "You look so much like him."

I was unsure of what to say.

"I mean, you're much prettier, but..."

We both laughed a little. I took his hand.

"How are you really? I'm so sorry that you had to... I'm so sorry. At first, I was in shock. Finding out I had a brother. And a twin! And that you were alive. I questioned you for leaving, him for being absolutely evil, and...myself for Wesley being absolutely evil and I was half of him. I know I'm rambling."

Jude hugged me.

"No. No, Willa. I've missed you. I apologize for missing out on your life and your magic. You have so many around you who love and adore you. That gives me comfort."

I squeezed him back.

"Dad."

He picked me up off of my feet and spun me around twice. "My darling daughter!"

I pulled back and we were both smiling through tears.

"I would never let Wesley's actions be a guide or comparison to your character. As I wouldn't want anyone to compare me to my mother."

"Never, Willa. And thank you." He let go of me and wiped his eyes. "Now, I'm going home. I offered to drive Marita to the airport tomorrow. I hope you'll be keen to my visiting you in the states?"

"I'd like that." We hugged again. "I'll see you out."

Twenty-Five

WILLA

David had already left for Lust. Alder and Micah watched me attempt to get ready. My emotions were scattered, excited and amping up. I only had a towel wrapped around me because my brain floated in limbo.

"I just went blank. What am I doing? What should I wear? Why the fuck am I so frazzled?"

Alder stopped my pacing and held on to my shoulders.

"You're overthinking it, darling."

"Yeah, David will like anything you put on. You're perfect." Micah winked. "I think you should go commando."

I scoffed. "What? Are you serious?"

He raised his perfect eyebrows. "I know it's something you wouldn't usually do, and he would never expect it."

Alder growled as he reached down and squeezed my ass through the terry cloth. "Oh my god, the thought has me painfully turned on."

I hummed and kissed Alder, letting our tongues dance and tease. I was getting wet imagining how erotic it would feel walking through the club without underwear on.

"Hmm, yes. I think I'll go sans panties. Good idea, Micah."

Alder let go of me and went to the closet. He pulled out a black faux leather dress with spaghetti straps that I had never worn before.

"This," he said with a spark in his eye.

Micah clicked his tongue. "David better realize what a lucky vampire he is."

I dropped the towel to the floor and went to him. I guided his hand to one of my breasts.

"Don't ever forget, I'm yours and Alder's first. Always."

Micah kissed me and I had to force myself to pull away because things were getting intense.

"Alright, boys. I seriously have to get ready."

Micah sighed and plopped down onto the bed as I went into the bathroom to finish.

ALDER HAD a limo pick us up. Us being me, Alder, Micah, Harris, and Trace. I laughed to myself picturing Trace in a vampire sex club. She was more modest than me and as far as I knew, she and Harris were still taking things somewhat slow. My best friend would have told me otherwise. I could tell she was excited though.

Harris took her straight to the bar when we went inside. I followed because I needed a drink badly. Micah ordered me a whiskey sour, and I threw it back. A pretty woman with a short brown pixie cut and gold mini dress approached us. Alder kissed her cheek and introduced her to me.

"Willa, this is Aleksandra. She's my preferred donor and was instrumental in Micah's training."

Micah smiled at her. I shook her hand, which allowed me to feel her energy without her noticing. She was sincere, pure of heart, and had a fun edgy personality. Perfect, I thought.

132

"Thank you for your help. I truly appreciate you."

I noticed Micah touch his abdomen. I leaned into Aleksandra's ear. "Why don't you take these two for a little drink."

She offered her hands to Alder and Micah. "Shall we?"

They accepted and I watched her lead them through a black door. I ordered one more drink and finally felt ready to find David.

Like magic, I felt a nose nuzzle the back of my neck and my whole body vibrated. Blood simultaneously rushed to my face and my clit, and I turned around to see David's wicked grin.

"You're blushing, babe."

I wanted to grab his cock right there, but we needed to get out of the main area of the bar. He read my mind. He tucked my arm through his and took me through the black door.

We made our way to the end of the hall where a bouncer let us into what I immediately knew was David's office.

"This is where I work." He kept walking across the room to another door and stopped before opening it. "This is where I play."

The walls and floor were deep, seductive purple. A bed dominated one side. A bed made for BDSM with straps and plenty of cushiony pillows. That didn't surprise me. I had seen pictures of these beds before. What was new to me was a table that sat in front of a plush blue sofa. It was at least seven feet long and looked like a coffee table, but it was a cage. The top was padded and had straps like the bed. I was enthralled. I ran a hand over the red leather surface on top.

"What is this called?"

"A cage table. It's new."

A thrill ran through me. "New? You mean, you haven't used it before?"

"No. I bought it for us."

It was so silly, I felt special for him buying a BDSM sex table with me in mind.

David waited as I continued to take it all in. I looked up at the mirrors on the ceiling. I slowly circled the room then came to stand in front of him. I tried not to think too much, because I didn't want him to know my every move. I slid my fingers under the lapels of his suit jacket and pushed it off of his shoulders. He wasn't wearing a tie, so I began unbuttoning the crisp white cotton shirt. He didn't say a word.

"I want you naked."

He obeyed and undressed the rest of the way. It was time to continue what we had started in his bedroom on his birthday.

"From now on, it's only yes or no. Do you understand?"

His chest heaved with a sigh of anticipation. "Yes."

"On your knees."

He complied. I looked over to the table. I wasn't sure how it was used, but I was a smart girl. I could figure it out. I stood in front of him, just out of reach, and slid the top of my dress down so that he could see my bare breasts. My nipples were hard for him, and my pussy was drenched. The tips of his fangs showed behind parted lips. I turned my back to him and slowly shimmied the dress over my perky ass, and I heard him take in a sharp breath at the sight. My skin burned to have his hands on me, but...not yet.

I was edging myself just as much as I planned on edging David. I let him watch me walk to the side of the table. I bent over it to tease him, pressing my breasts against the cold surface. It was the perfect height and I imagined him pounding into me from behind. David groaned when he read my mind. Oh, the fun I was having. I stood back up and turned to see him. His cock was so hard and long and ready, but...not yet.

I went to him and thumbed his bottom lip. David growled when I put it into his mouth. He sucked and licked it, and now I moaned. My wetness barely dripped down the inside of my thighs. I knew he saw it. I couldn't help myself. I panted. I needed to get off. It felt like I could quite possibly orgasm just by taking a few steps.

"Do you want me?"

"Yes," David hissed.

"Get in the cage," I demanded.

David crawled on hands and knees and got inside.

"Have you ever been in a cage?"

"No."

"Do you like it?"

"No."

My ankles were positioned in front of him, and he tentatively reached a hand between the bars. His fingers grazed up my calf to the back of my knee. My body wanted to melt, but I stepped just out of reach. He made a noise of disappointment. Almost a whimper. When I got on top of the table, I looked over the edge and David was gripping the bars. I laid on my back and let my arm fall over the side.

"Lick my fingers, David."

He licked and sucked and groaned. I pulled them away and slid them over my pussy.

"I'm touching myself, David."

I knew he loved it when I said his name. His breaths were loud beneath me.

"Hold onto the bars. I don't want you to come."

My fingers flattened against my swollen clit, and I circled faster. My legs spread further apart and my ass grinded against the leather.

"I'm thinking about you finger fucking me, David."

I imagined his fingers sliding inside me and I shuddered and panted as the orgasm hit and I came hard. I heard him whisper, fuck. I moved to sit, kneeling beside the cage so that I could see his face. He was staring upwards and looked thoroughly frustrated. Energy vibrated in my hands, and I reached one inside the cage to grab David's cock. He tensed up and latched a hand on my wrist to increase the stroking. I squeezed.

"No."

"Yes," he whined.

I let go. "No."

He closed his eyes. When he heard the door creak open, his head snapped up.

"Do you want to escape?"

"Yes."

"Hmm...okay. Lay down on the top."

He did and his eyes never left me.

"Do you want me to let you come?"

"Yes."

"Not yet."

David looked up at the mirrors and blew out a hard breath between his lips and I took some time to admire him. He really was perfectly made. I thought about his guarded heart and how he had seemed to let me in. At least I hoped I was right. He turned his head to look at me. His eyes glowed. I strapped his ankles and wrists down as he watched. I concentrated the energy still swirling inside down to my palms and they glowed as I began to rub them over his chest. He hummed with pleasure.

"Thank you for this table, David."

My fingers traced the v-lines on both hips and when I wrapped them around his cock, he gasped. My strokes were slow. He looked at me and bared his fangs. I increased the pace, and he dropped his head back on the padding. David gripped the edges of the table and growled as cum spurted across his belly. We were both satisfied. I left the straps on while I cleaned him up. After, I released him.

"You may sit up."

David's long legs hung down and I stepped in between his knees. I ruffled his hair back in place and he grinned with no fangs. I lifted his lip.

"Gone so soon? Don't you want a taste?"

He hesitated. "May I speak?"

"Yes."

"Yes, I want a taste. I want to taste you more than anything, Willa, but not here. Not like this."

David was showing me how deeply he cared. He wanted that intimate act to be private. Special.

"Okay." I kissed him and he sweetly kissed me back. "Can I tell you something that may scare you?"

He grinned again. "Yes."

"I love you, my wild thing."

He snatched me around the waist and crushed me against his chest. His nose was in my hair, and he mumbled into my ear.

"Babe, I...I'm so lucky. I can't believe I'm so lucky."

I leaned back a little. "Well, do you feel the same?"

"Yes! Yes, of course. You keep surprising me, you know. I fell in love with the woman of my dreams. Literally." David caressed my cheek. "I loved you a little more with each one. I know you don't remember every time we were together, but I do. I saw your soul and I knew you would accept me for me. It's going to be very hard for me when you have to go."

His mouth turned down in a sad pout, so I gave him little kisses all over his face. He laughed and squirmed when I poked his side.

"No. no, no. No tickling, woman."

"No sad stuff tonight. I had to tell you because I wanted you to know you are loved. So much. I'm claiming you."

"Oh, you are?"

"Mmm hmm. But I won't tell anyone how whipped you are."

"Whipped? Oh, you minx."

David jumped off of the table and I ran. He easily caught me and threw me on the bed. Then he threw my dress at me.

"We're getting dressed. I want to buy you a drink at my bar."

ALDER AND MICAH were already at the bar drinking whiskey. I went to them and quickly kissed both of them on the mouth before returning to David's arms.

"How do you like Lust?" Micah asked with a wink.

"It's great." I tightened my hold around David's waist. "Be sure to tell the owner I can't wait to come back the next time we are in London."

"He eagerly awaits your return," David mumbled into my hair as he kissed the top of my head.

I peeled myself away from David when Harris and Trace walked up. Trace came to stand next to me and whispered in my ear.

"This place is wild."

"Oh, yeah? What have you two been doing?"

We turned to lean on the bar, so the others didn't listen in. Trace's eyebrows went up.

"Well, I fed Harris while we watched two vampires fucking. Willa! I've never!"

I laughed. "Was it hot?"

"Oh my god, yes! All of the fangs and sucking and I've never seen so many positions."

"Wow. I guess I haven't thought about what it's like for true vampire couples. How they feel every sensation so much more than we do. And the stamina. I bet it's off the charts."

"Willa, it makes me want to be turned. Like, soon."

I believed Trace was born to be a vampire. "I know you're ready."

"And I know you're not. I'll be the guinea pig," she joked. "Harris and I are going to have a serious discussion about it when we get back to New Orleans."

I hugged my best friend. "I'm so happy for a night with no drama...and lots of sex."

We both laughed and everyone else looked at us. Micah slid a hand over my hip. "I love hearing your laugh. I want to hear it every day for the rest of my life."

I knew he was thinking about what happened before with Cateline and then Wesley. I held his face. "Do you know how much I love you?"

He rolled his eyes.

"I'm serious. I thought you were gone. I thought my own flesh and blood ended you and I didn't know if I could live with myself if he had."

"Willa, don't you ever say that. I know. I know how you feel about me. I felt you in that room with me. Even when darkness was around me and I thought I had slipped away completely. I felt you there. Damn, I love you."

He hugged me hard, and I knew everything would be okay. For now...

Acknowledgments

I have always been fascinated with vampires. Many of my favorite movies are about them. Throw witches into the cauldron and it takes the story to a whole new level.

Thank you to my friend, Michelle, for asking me to write a tale of best friend witches with vampire boyfriends. "Falling for Fangs" was only the beginning.

Another big thanks to Marita Woywod Crandle for writing the inspiring book "New Orleans Vampires: History and Legends". She also graciously gave me her permission to mention Boutique du Vampyre and Potions Lounge in "Falling for Fangs" and agreed to being an even bigger character in this story.

This tale may be good, but it wouldn't be great without the best editor on the planet, Brandi Zelenka. And cover designer Angela Haddon worked absolute magic!

Finally, love and thanks always to my family who provide never ending support. XOXO

About the Author

Ginger Lee, romance novelist and dark poet, spends her days raising her daughter, traveling with her husband, and attending concerts with friends. She is an avid reader and coffee & vampire enthusiast who collects art, movies, Monster High Dolls and oddities. In her free time, she enjoys walks through the neighborhood, thrift store shopping and watching Sanditon. Ginger loves to connect with other authors/readers and the writing community on social media.

Playlist

Trouble – Cold Play
Sex, Drugs, Etc. – Beach Weather
All I Want – Kodaline
Nobody Gets Me – SZA
Where Are U Now – Justin Bieber, Jack U, Skrillex & Diplo
I'm Yours – Isabel LaRosa
Middle of the Night – Elley Duhe
Love Brand New – Bob Moses
On My Knees – Rufus du Sol
Run Away to Mars – TALK
Head Over Heels – Tears for Fears
Holdin On – Bazzi
Fire for You – Cannons
Long Nights – Hazy & CMAXLINK

How to Contact Ginger Lee

- Email: gleewrites@gmail.com
- Website: gleewrites.com
- www.twitter.com/glee_writes
- www.instagram.com/authorgingerlee
- https://ko-fi.com/gingerlee
- https://allauthor.com/author/gleewrites/.
- www.goodreads.com/gleewrites
- www.facebook.com/gingerweather
- Amazon: